deep overstock

#17: Beekeeping

July 2022

AGRI - BEES/BEEKEEPING

EDITORIAL

EDITORS-IN-CHIEF: Mickey Collins & Robert Eversmann

MANAGING EDITORS: Michael Santiago & Z.B. Wagman

POETRY: Melissa Kerman & Jihye Shin

PROSE: Michael Santiago & Z.B. Wagman

COVER: *Spring Day* by Unknown, 1900

CONTACT: editors@deepoverstock.com
deepoverstock.com

ON THE SHELVES

continued...

Letter from the Editors

Dearest Readers,

Are you buzzing with excitement over this issue? Can you not wait to read the honeyed words that our contributors have written? Ready to comb through and find the sweet nectar that resides within?

This issue we have queen bees, nurse bees, mason bees, Buddha bees, bees in fairy tales, bees in fall, bees in winter, beekeepers, and honey by the gallonful.

It has always been our pleasure to read all of the different submissions we receive. This issue was no different. However, we received so many great submissions we have put together our biggest issue yet. We feel like queen bees of the hive, with drones bringing offering after offering to feed our fat rumps so that we may continue to lay little bee eggs in the way of these journals. So thank you, dear contributors. And thank you readers for picking up this issue, as heavy as it may be.

And thank you bees! Bees do so many great things, it's no wonder that they're so busy all of the time. Without bees humankind would likely have starved. Go out there and plant some flowers so bees can keep being themselves and doing what they do. But first, help yourself to these poems and short stories.

After all of that, consider submitting to our 18th issue: Old Favorites, in which we are seeking pieces for any of our past 17 themes (including this one, if you feel so inspired after reading these pieces).

We will bee with you always,

Deep Overstock Editors

Temporarily Floating

by Yuan Changming

I am the little bee
He put on His hook
To be kissed or swallowed
By an unknown fish

Many trout are swimming around
I have no idea which one of them
He intends to take out of the stream
The only thing I hear is His laughter
Echoing along the tightened line

bees

by Mark DeCarteret

I peek into where
we keep them

too weak now
but to lean in

nearly kneeling
at worship

only cleared to
speak of them

in these news
leaks & hearsay

I've had to swear
off from honeyed lips

Ringling City, Where Bees Practice for the Circus

by Jan Ball

Fascinated all my life by acrobatic bees,
and honey-dependent, I wanted to write
a poem about them, then realized
that my elusive subject was right under my nose,
literally, in and out of the hollow red cedar tree
at the center of our Sarasota condo complex:
a swarm of 150,000 bees moved in practicing
their circus acts in full daylight
          before they enter the hive.

After several weeks of swatting the twirling bees,
and concern that dead tree limbs might smash
our windows like a Florida hurricane, the apiarists
we called in for advice confer and decide to move
the acrobats at night when they are less agitated.

Their queen lures them into manufactured bee boxes
with pollen cocktails, then the apiarists transfer them
to rural Myaka, anticipating that the bees
can practice their acts there without annoying
the elderly people in our community.

In the next few days itinerant scavenger bees
fly in looking for roustabout work.
They are disappointed to see that the circus
that they'd read about in the journal: Acrobatic Bees,
has moved. They'd hoped to audition for the special
disappearing six honeycomb act.

Dusting
by Ryan Clinesmith

I'm sitting on the porch.—Bees out of nowhere,
the UPS guy says, "It's a swarm, scary."

First I heard them, a loud rubbing engine
dusting the sky like a sunlit orb or a dark bubble

lifted out of string and rubber without the oily chrome.
Only blondish density, and fear, imagining

I was one, part of the airborne school,
peppered by their ire. We fear all bugs these days,

"Scary!" we say, thinking what it must be like
to be inside them and have them inside us.

Sunday Baroque

by Ryan Clinesmith

The silhouette of a ridge
half-clouded by morning fog
makes me think of

scorched grass in early fall
hemmed by leaves turning so fast
I can watch them redden, change

like corn or bamboo,——
the mind too
watching white-blossomed oregano,

bees, flying ants, a moth,
it's only when they've all flown off
that the signs of endings become apparent;

bees dead in the quad.
All I want to do is throw the frisbee

while the light catches it
curving to my target,
but there's no one waiting.

The good thing is, I've accepted it.
Spoken to grandma and she agrees
the earth is done with us. All we can do is sit,

watch the feral cats or sun
unveil itself as dew
in growing heat evaporates.

crescent dance
by Jihye Shin

(To be read in a looping figure eight pattern, as a mobius strip)

absconding hive
after the swarm

                                                  :orient:

nectar death --
"not born, but rather becomes"
              dearth
ocellus; oculus; ocelli open

Moving the Hive
by Sara Eddy

Only one hive made it
through this furious winter
of subzeroes and wind chill
bitter disputes and
marital strife; they were
the hardiest, I guess,
the colony with a queen
bent on survival,
in mad love with her brood.
After dividing and divisions
we agreed I'd keep the bees
and move them down the road
to a friend's garden: wildflowers,
mulberry trees, peace.
So I smoke this last hive
and talk to them gently:
I tell them they're strong.
I stop up their entrances,
and strap the hive together,
then lift it, heavy with buzz,
into the back of my car.
It's not far, I say: you'll be
fine, you'll be fine. Finally
in their new green world I lay a spray
of pine in front of the entrance,
and let them free: as the workers
leave the hive, they crawl
through the needles, an unfamiliar
must-smelling maze,
and they pay attention–
they live with intention–
and memorize the way back
to their new life.

Bee Yard
by Sara Eddy

I've let the yard go.
There's still grass, yes, but bit
by bit it steps aside for dandelions
and violets, creeping vines
with purple flowers, baby bluets
and buttercups. It is as if I'm
allowing space for one small
flower per bee, inviting them
to my yard for a drink.
The neighbors whose lawn is perfect,
who mow 3 times a week in the summer
and polish their driveway after
every scant snow in winter
are affronted; they barely speak to me
and they watch the dandelion heads
spill their seed into the air–
floaty spun sugar bombs settling down
to mark their blank canvas.
But I'm smug; I don't care.
My yard is a motley expressionist mess
a glorious garish foolishness
and given time, it will feed the world.

Fall Harvest
by Sara Eddy

I leave them stores for the winter,
gallons of honey and a thousand
golden pockets of pollen
gleaming in the dark of the hive
nourishing the workers
through the long cold.
But then I take my due,
the honey supers so heavy
my knees begin to buckle.
Sweetness is a heavy load
pulling at my gut. It's easier
to cut it with sour—goat cheese
or ricotta—a balance against
the sting of the nectar.
But I'm old enough to take it straight
when I want it, like the time
you surprise kissed me on the mouth
and we found new worlds of honey.
At home, I slice open the cells
and spin the honey out,
an aureate ribbon piling up on itself,
spun through with light and air.
The smell is rich insect life
and potential, stretching out over eons,
eternal and real, and I fill my cup to the brim.

Saint of beekeepers and beggars

by Jennifer Clark

You were golden at birth, Ambrose,
a swarm of bees settled on your face,
leaving behind a single drop of honey.

We've heard this before, bees landing
on the breath of baby Zeus and Bacchus,
Virgil and Plato, foretelling sweetness of speech.

As sermons drip from your honeyed tongue,
we gather nectar, beat our wings ragged
to build the kingdom. Still, winter arrives,

this season of sadness in which we find
no flowers to forage. Unlike our bumbly
brothers and sisters, we do not hibernate.

In the hive of Christ, we stay awake, bodies
pressed together, shivering, generating heat
for our mother of honeycomb, candles, and bees.

Is everything we do for the queen?
The good news: we have more honey than we need.
Time now to share the sweet. Why is this so hard to do?

Megachilidae

by Estée Arts Crenshaw

As it chews
through
the nursery
loaves,
hatching brood
tunnels through
an immaculate darkness
immured with
careful clippings.

Its birth into
the light bristles
with a certainty
unknown to us
who wake
into an opacity
so densely vacuous
that we subsist
on sifted memories.

Sorrow
by Estée Arts Crenshaw

A firstborn sorrow buffers its descendants
In the same way early bees in a hive
Smear propolis into every crack
Encasing the queen in darkness

We Watch and Wait
by Lydia Gwyn

We've suited up into our white coveralls, gloves, hard hats, elasticized netting. Tom says he feels like a volunteer firefighter on a last-minute call, pulling on equipment, rushing out the door. My suit is stained with splotches of honey and propolis and old smoker residue. In three years, I've never bothered to wash it.

The swarm of bees is in our easement this time, just a few feet off the ground in a tangle of honeysuckle vines and dead elephant ear branches. We caught this same swarm last week when it was twenty feet up a pine tree. We'd had to pull out the ladder we use for cleaning the second-floor gutters of our home to reach them then. We shook the bees into their new hive that day, but they didn't stay.

This time we watch and wait. Thousands of the bees still fill the air and their buzzing is intoxicating like the white noise machines we used to put our children to sleep when they were babies. Static like puffy pillows filling the air behind a closed door.

The swarm is forming a bearded ball when a red truck drives up and pulls into our easement. The window is down, and I recognize the driver. He's introduced himself twice before.

"I'm Seth Campbell," the man says. "I own the farm behind your house." He has white hair and aviator glasses. He wears overalls. His farm is hundreds of acres, and his house is nestled somewhere in the woods where we can't see. Sometimes my son crosses the barbed wire and hikes around his land looking for morels and shadows hiding behind trees. Seth asks about the swarm, says he's seen a few before, knows the queen is in there in the center of everything.

"If you see a cow wandering around here, let me know," he says, "I've got a loose one."

I tell him I see his cows all the time but none outside his pasture. I tell him they come up to the fence and watch our kids play in the yard, my daughter swinging high on the tire swing. "They're beautiful," I say, "especially the ones with the long horns."

We exchange more pleasantries. Seth watches for a while as the swarm tightens, and when the bees have clustered completely, he leaves and we get to work.

I hold back branches while Tom clips the honeysuckle. We move slowly, nothing sudden. We grab vines before they hit the ground. We whisper. Tom clips. This branch, that. "It's like dismantling a bomb," he says.

When all the honeysuckle is cleared away, I hold the main branch containing the swarm, while Tom saws. He uses a Japanese rasp saw with teeth as fine as sand. He makes smooth, almost soundless motions, and I think of him then pressing me against our bedroom wall the night before. Kissing the back of my neck, hands fitted into the frames of my hips.

We have loved each other for twenty years this year.

A few bees walk over my hand and the swarm sways with Tom's movement. When the cut is clean, we lower the branch—Tom holding one end and I holding the other—and place the swarm on top of a nuc box fitted with four frames of wax foundation.

We hope this time the bees will crawl inside the box on their own. We hope they'll think it's their idea—this new home—and they'll stay this time. We leave everything as it is and decide to return at night.

Back in the house, I strip off my suit and gear and step into my writing studio, into a sound bath of binaural beats and subliminal flow states. I write for a while about hexagons and the waxy, sweet smell that bees infuse into everything they touch.

My children go in and out of the kitchen for snacks. A

movie begins and ends on the living room TV. For dinner, I make veggie burgers piled high with sliced avocado, tomatoes, olives, lettuce, cucumbers. The burgers are too thick for the kids' mouths. Before they eat, they smash them with the palms of their hands to thin them out.

At my daughter's bedtime, the two of us watch the old Steel Magnolias trailer on my phone. My daughter had wanted to know who Julia Roberts was. My son comes into the room and tells us there's a black cat with green eyes sitting in my garden. "It's covered in mud," he says, "and it doesn't have a collar." I tell him I've seen that cat many times before. I tell him the cat is feral and won't let anyone approach it. Both children now want to catch the cat. My daughter devises a plan for the morning that involves shaking a plastic container of Pounce cat treats. She names the cat Shadow. I put her to bed. I smoothe her hair. There are curls around her forehead that have been there since she was born. She stares into space, a thousand miles away, while I sing a song about mockingbirds.

Late that night once both children are sleeping, Tom and I return to the easement. The swarm has regrouped inside the nuc and turned off their collective minds for the night. I remove the empty branch and shut the lid, latch it in place, and Tom carries the nuc up to the hive stand in our yard. The new hive is right next to the old hive, which sleeps now with a new queen.

From the Impatient Beekeeper's Notebook

by Mary Salome

Sweet Time

Honey's timeless flow
mocks the clock's imperative
takes its own sweet time

On Making Frames

The keeping of bees
Becomes a carpenter's affair;
tonight, I'll wash the glue
not the honey
from my hair.

Solstice

Restless, knowing that
even the longest day casts
shadows on the hive

Tranquility
by Tom Barlow

The bees are laden with pollen
this time of year. I watch them
labor to rise, to carry their
bounty home. No malaise there,

no sense of opportunities lost,
ninety days doing what they were
born for, a life fulfilled.
Retirement is not part of their

contract, of course, never this
hammock, never these gin rickeys,
never this poolside breeze in Cabo,
never this worry over a letter

from the IRS. My wife obsesses
about the flower garden back home.
That persistent pain behind my knee,
hopefully not a blood clot.

The house needs a new roof, both
cats are fifteen, my brother voted
for Trump, and these bees can
just fly away from it all.

Am I such a sad man as to covet the
vacant mind, the clear sky? Wicked as
I might be, I would never trap such peace
under an empty highball glass, or ten.

In The Care of Bees
by Stella Bauer

I discovered the beehive when I was nine. I was playing hide and seek with Rebecca and stumbled across the little nest in the woods that were the boarding house's yard. It was no bigger than a football when I first found it, the hive barely buzzing with its residents. I remember being scared at first, afraid that it would attack me, and I would have to spend the night in the nurse's office. But as I sat there looking at the hive, the bees continued to lazily visit the flowers surrounding us. They brushed up against my limbs but didn't sting, simply looked to see if I had any nectar to give. And then they buzzed away.

I won that game of hide and seek. It was then that I discovered the bees, and I had a secret place. A sanctuary. I started escaping there every game of hide and seek or when I needed to run from my tutor's lessons. Or if I needed to burrow away from the barbs of the other girls in my class. No one ever found me, no one was ever brave enough to breach the boundaries of the bees.

When I was twelve, I started eating my lunches and spending my free time between classes with the bees. Rachel and I had stopped being friends and none of the other girls seemed to want to invite me into their groups. Not that I minded, the bees became my company. They never made rude comments about my hair or made fun of me when I stumbled around my words. They buzzed and listened patiently to my day. They drank the nectar of flowers and rested on my open hands and bare feet. I started stealing wildflower seeds from the grounds keeper's cottage and bringing it to the bees. Under my care, in our friendship, the beehive nearly doubled in size, bringing new bees with it.

Bees will build their hives around anything. I discovered this when I was fourteen, I accidentally left a cup by the hive before a long weekend. I had eaten lunch with the bees and lost track of the time, and in my rush my drinking glass fell at the base of the tree the beehive grew on. When I returned to the bees, three days later, they had started to grow their home around the cup. The holes of their nest covered half of the cup, the hive forming and around the obstruction. But it wasn't really an obstruction to them, it was an opportunity for expansion. They persevered, thrived, and grew off what I had given them, like the wildflowers I planted two years previous. I liked that a little piece of me remained with them, around them, in their home.

This little trick came in handy when I was sixteen. Rachel's book went missing one morning. Or rather, I had stolen Rachel's book. I overheard her telling Sandra that I was unusual and creepy, that I spent more time outside in the woods than inside. I heard her say that if I spent more time inside than maybe I wouldn't be at the bottom of our class. Rachel said that she was ashamed that she was ever my friend. I went to the bees and cried that day. They enveloped around me in a swarm, wrapping me with their soft bodies and comforting hums. Rachel was my friend; she was always nice and didn't mind that I was quiet or struggled with my sentences. We played together; we ate together. Without me and her playing hide and seek I wouldn't have found the bees. The bees who now rested around me. Their buzzes became a song, a call. Protection.

I stole Rachel's book that night, she left it out on her bedside table. She needed it for a presentation the next day and stayed up late reading it. When she woke up the next morning to find it was gone, she immediately blamed me, but they didn't find it in my trunk or with my belongings. What the school didn't know is that I had already sneaked out to the beehive that night. The bees were covering the book completely as Rachel failed her presentation.

It's a shame what happened to Rachel next.

She had followed me into the woods that afternoon, she was looking for the book. She knew that I had taken it, she told me as much. She barged into the alcove with the bee's nest, which had grown to cover the entire trunk of the tree and the ground beneath its shade. Rachel found me sitting near the base of the hive, my legs half covered with bees. Her book sat open on the ground, already overtaken by a swarm building their waxen home atop it. I remember that she froze. I imagine it to be quite a sight. Me and all the bees there. Her book, the evidence of her work and my crime open in front of her. She started screaming at me.

Rachel didn't listen to the bees growing louder around her. At the swarms rising to double her height, at the bees forming a barrier between me and her. Rachel's mistake was not leaving. She had to step forward to try and claim the book. I'll never forget the look Rachel had as the bees turned their stingers on her. They moved with a vengeance to protect their home. To protect what I had given them. To protect me. Rachel fell to the ground, terror in her eyes and her mouth wide open with a scream on her lips. A scream that came because the bees had already rushed into her throat.

I don't know how long Rachel took to die, but I know the bees took hours to calm down. I cried. Not for Rachel, but for the bees who had given their lives to me just as I had given myself to them. Once the bees stopped attacking Rachel, they started to build around her. They built inside her. She became another gift that I gave the bees, a new place to find a home.

The school went into a tizzy over Rachel going missing. I was questioned of course, but they could never find a reason to convict me. They never found the body. That secret remains in an alcove of honey and wildflowers. A secret in my care, and in the care of the bees.

Final Time
by John Davis

He the hairy-footed flower bee
goes around comes around
gingery brown buzzes a hum
over lungworts, dead nettles

bumps from his shallow hollow nest
to find a mate before he dies
wanting a new hum
that will wrap him in pollen

far from humorous bravado
of wings vibrating the air
which is what we want:
a final hymn unembellished

so we won't look the other way.

Buddha Bee
by John Davis

Such buzz the honey bee:
small wonder Miles Davis
lived in a bee-loud glen
when he played his horn
let his wings vibrate
from bee balm
to marsh blazing star.

Scissor Bee's First Day

by John Davis

Here is the light he was born into
fragile green glow
already in wind and leaves
day winding down
To open a tunnel of air
To hover above the clover
homeless in love
with the touch of earth
To waver in brush and weeds
Invincible flit of flight

Save the Bees

by Timothy Arliss OBrien

The pollinators sing,
and the perennials dance through their short little lifespan.

The bridge takes us over the water,
And my two little wheels gift me freedom
and grant me an overwhelming sense of calm.

I wish that nature would take back over, and we could lay down
and relinquish the earth unto her.
(Her being mother Gaia.)

My friends, the bees, don't ask for much,
And we know deep in our souls that we owe them
the world.

Once in a while, I stare at the sky and
Try not to think.
Don't do it.

Think of nothing.

And while you are at it
Start the undoing,

Of the overthinking, yes,
But of all the tropes they told us we had to fit into,
of hopelessness,
And all the little things that send your brain into overdrive
And so quickly caused a full system collapse.

There is so much to look forward to.
We need you here,

And please,
Save yourself

So you can help us
Save the bees.

Honey

by Stephanie Fluckey

Honey never goes bad. My husband always bought bear shaped honey. He called me Honey, or Hun when he was looking over the paper wanting my opinion—the one that agreed with his.

I prefer jars. When the honey solidifies, dense enough to be hung from a chain like amber, it's easier to scoop out. I cannot get my knife into the little arms and legs. The plastic bear's bottom is tattooed with don't microwave, but everyone does, except him. He tosses the bear—clogged limbs and all—into the trash.

On the grocery shelf there is clover honey, and organic honey (what is inorganic honey—mechanical bees?) I remember my husband telling me honey would help my allergies—local honey—but he always came home with the honey-bear from a city hundreds of miles away.

In the morning, he used his middle finger to wipe the honey from the corner of his mouth. I would pass him a napkin and little shreds of paper would stick to his fingers, like the dots on his face after a rough shave. His chin is like a Kandinsky color study, the poster of which used to be on my friend's kitchen wall—when we were both single and happy. She married, I married, she's still married. I used to love that painting.

I chose a large jar of honey with a wide mouth. I collected a few more things, I picked out ten apples, then put six back. A small package of chicken, salad, coffee creamer, bagels.

I grabbed the honey from the basket to lift it onto the conveyor belt and it slipped from my hands. It smashed open and oozed onto the floor. I was tempted to push the tip of my shoe into it. I wanted something to stick to.

"Don't worry, we'll clean it up—do you need us to grab another one?" the clerk asked.

I looked up. "No, I don't even like honey," I said.

Inexplicable
by Karla Linn Merrifield

 When the yellow jacket stung
my hand, it died.
I plucked out its stinger
along with a portion of its posterior.

He bequeathed me his asshole,
his apian F-you,
and crash dove. He bit the sand
and I left a footstep in the trail.

For three days, fingers, palm,
wrist remained swollen, throbbed.
Only my opposable thumb was spared
to function normally. Not much help.

Antihistamines performed well.
I slept, and slept some more.
I had woozy, broken-winged dreams
about paratrooper bees.

In one scene the former executed
a widespread populations collapse;
there was famine in the lands of honey.
In another restless, fervid scenario,

bees plummeted from dark skies,
bombing bare-headed passersby
across the Arkansas Ozarks into Louisiana.
Thousands of striped insects flashed yellow

rings in mysterious defeat.
By Friday, I was able to properly
operate my computer mouse around
its pad, click on the Times headlines,

read clear-eyed on screen how
my hypoallergenic nightmares came true.

Squadrons of bees had struck again.
And again.

So much for opposable thumbs
and their digitized prowess online.
I may have recovered, but I will not
survive the next extinction.

The Fly
by Melissa Kerman

Yesterday afternoon The Fly followed me through my door
flying in with the wind because the wind flows with the
confidence of one who knows where to go
I, too, follow the wind when I crave an adventure
but The Fly couldn't have known that my home
has no treasure near, only disarray and disaster here

I inform The Fly that there are better places to explore
so I reopen my screen door but The Fly turns to my kitchen
past dishes I stole from my mother and phone charger from my
brother
bills informing me that my debt is higher and my car insurance
will expire,
a coffee-stained "Best Girlfriend" mug gifted from a now-ex
boyfriend,
which I tell The Fly I still use because of my affinity for
dramatic irony

That evening I would've invited The Fly to sleep in my bed
but my restlessness would've crushed him instead
Someone like me is better off alone, I tell The Fly
but since he's inspected my home, I suspect
he doesn't need me to explain why

In the morning I found The Fly in a frenzy
Slamming into the wall and spazzing after each fall
His tempo became slow as he buzzed like a dull radio
I swayed him towards the window but he refused to go
Until he dropped to the floor and The Fly moved no more

When I mourned I wondered if he passed because of me
though I warned The Fly that my company is poor quality
Maybe he meant to commence the beginning of his end
Maybe he understood and I misunderstood The Fly
Maybe he recognized that within my presence he'd die

The Queen Bee

by Melissa Kerman

Steven broke up with Kelly after she was stung by the bee.

I can confirm this because I was there. According to Kelly's version of the story, she broke up with Steven *before* the bee sting.

I don't know what I expected when I called her out on the discrepancy.

"I was going to do it. Before the bee stung me, before Steven laughed, I was literally about to do it, but then I had to tell him off. I started screaming and he started screaming back, because–well, you remember. Anyway, the point is that he beat me to the words, but in my mind, I had already broken up with him. So, yeah, I'm allowed to tell people that I did."

"That's not how the world works," I responded. "Doing things in your head isn't equivalent to doing them in real life. People keep asking me what happened."

"One, you're not my PR rep, so you don't need to answer. You can say you don't know instead of trying to gain clout off of my business. Two, why are you so concerned about how I chronicle *my* breakup?

"Kelly, I–"

"It's my life, not yours. You're supposed to have my back. You're a shitty friend," she snapped. "If you want to fuck Steven, just say that."

Then she hung up. That was last week. Kelly and I hadn't spoken until she called me yesterday.

"I've been reflecting on the breakup. And the relationship," she said, as soon as I picked up. "I think Steven's gay. It's the only logical reason why we ended. He needed an 'out' from the relationship. That's why he started laughing when the bee stung me. He knew I'd freak out and he'd have an excuse to walk. Everything makes sense."

"You are delusional." I hung up.

Then she unfollowed me on Instagram.

"I heard you laughed when the bee stung Kelly," Rebecca said at brunch, three days prior to Kelly's and my last conversation, "and didn't chime in when they started fighting. You knew Steven was gonna break up with her that day, didn't you?"

"It's really not my place to discuss Kelly's love life."

Rebecca tilted her head. "So why were you there?"

"Because she invited me! Why the fuck would I go otherwise? You think Steven told me to ambush their date? What the hell, Rebecca?"

The family seated beside us stared.

Rebecca took a long sip of her drink. "You're getting awfully defensive for someone who supposedly had zero involvement in the situation."

"Because I'm not sure what you're trying to get out of this. And you're, like, the fifth person to ask me what happened, but I'm not relevant to the story. The afternoon would've transpired the same had I not been there."

I lifted the menu. Brunch had been my idea. Rebecca wasn't enthusiastic when I texted, but I knew she wouldn't decline mimosas. "You gonna order anything? The french toast here is amazing."

Rebecca downed her drink and threw cash on the table. "I would, but I gotta go. Long workday tomorrow. Nice catching up with you, though."

She left before I could answer. I would've told her that

we'll plan something soon, but she didn't imply that she wanted to.

Kelly, Rebecca, and Jessica stopped writing in the group chat we'd maintained since college.

"I think they created a new one. Without me. Yesterday Jessica posted a picture on Facebook of them at dinner."

My sister and I strolled through Zara, stopping in front of a sale rack.

"You think this would make my ass look good?" She held a magenta bodycon dress.

"Are you even listening to me? I'm telling you I've been exiled from my friend group and all you can think about is your ass?"

She rolled her eyes. "I am listening. Actually, you just sounded exactly like Kelly. No wonder you two are best friends."

"Well, if you were paying attention, you would've heard that Kelly has decided not to be my friend anymore. The other girls, too. With me, I mean. They're all still friends."

"Who cares? I never liked those bitches. You didn't do anything. You never do, yet they've been ganging up on you since college. That's high school behavior yet you're all twenty-four. Ridiculous."

I stopped walking, catching myself in a mirror. "You know… they do kind of gang up on me. But why is this the inciting incident for them to shun me?"

"Because this is the first time you're defending yourself." She tossed the dress on a table. "Let's go. Everything here is ugly."

I couldn't sleep that night. My dream awoke me. Nightmare, really, because Kelly, Steven, and I were back in Central Park, on the infamous day, but Steven didn't break up with Kelly. He told her that the only way to fix their fractured relationship was to have a threesome with me. Kelly started crying. Steven and I had sex anyway, right there on Kelly's quilt. Hundreds of bees swarmed our bodies and coated us in honey. Passerbys formed a circle. Kelly recorded the scene on her iPhone and posted it on the internet.

I woke up sweating and enraged. There was no way I'd fall back asleep, so I grabbed my notepad.

Three things define Kelly:
1) She has never been dumped.
2) She is the Queen Bee of our group, and the world.
3) She is allergic to bees.

These details had to be connected.

I circled item one. Kelly never dated men who hadn't already fallen in love with her because every man she met fell in love with her. Granted, she's shaped like a Coke bottle and her face resembles a China doll, but men don't solely want to bang Kelly–they want to marry her. Kelly entrances everyone, which brings me to point two.

Hilarious, I scribbled onto my pad. I met Kelly the third day of my sophomore year. She sat in our dorm lounge, surrounded, as she recited a conversation she had with her history professor. The anecdote wouldn't have been half as riveting if someone other than Kelly told it. Kelly could joke about a car manual and the audience would roar.

Extroverted. I had walked into the lounge to fill my water bottle, and eavesdrop, because I wanted to see what the fuss was about. Kelly paused her tale to introduce herself and ask if I lived on the floor. She roomed with her two best friends, Jessica and Rebecca. They invited me out with them that night. I must've told thirty strangers my name because Kelly couldn't take a step without someone stopping her. Through her, my identity finally mattered.

Direct. In movies, the Queen Bee asserts her dominance through snark and aggression. It's the lid that covers the Queen Bee's boiling self-doubt, which threatens to overflow and tarnish the pot. Contrarily, Kelly's confidence isn't superficial. She doesn't need to boss people around because they *choose* to follow her.

The stereotypical Queen Bee's head is too far up her ass to advise her minions, let alone respect them. However, Kelly is a loyal friend. A frat guy called me fat after I rejected him. Not only did Kelly get him kicked out of his frat, but he ended up transferring schools. I'm still not sure what she did. I never questioned her powers.

Until now.

I never liked those bitches. You didn't do anything. You never do, yet they've been ganging up on you since college.

Do the girls gang up on me? I mean, sometimes they laugh at me. Like when I trip. They call me their "little klutz." They think my Russian doll collection is weird. And my "dad jokes." They insist on dressing me before evening plans because my fashion sense cannot be trusted. They hate my sweater vests. And Birkenstocks. They really hate my Birkenstocks.

My heart beat faster. I called my sister.

"I need to ask you something. Please answer honestly."

She groaned. "What could you possibly need to ask me at four in the morning?"

"I want to know if I'm weird. Like, am I a weird person?"

"You woke me up at four AM to ask if I think you're weird?"

"Correct. Please answer."

"Yes. You are weird. Goodbye."

I rocked back and forth. "Oh my God," I murmured, squeezing my teddy bear, "They're cutting me off because I'm weird."

The knot in my stomach tightened, but not due to my potential conclusion. I gripped my notepad.

The situation still didn't feel resolved.

She is allergic to bees.

I used to think nothing terrified Kelly, not even three-hundred-pound club bouncers or cops. I credited that to her childhood with four older brothers. In May of our sophomore semester, though, as we lounged in the grass, a bee flew onto Kelly's cranberry vodka. She knocked over her red solo cup and screamed so loud that the entire campus must've heard. The bee chased Kelly and she began to sob, harder than Rebecca did after her boyfriend dumped her for a freshman.

"Relax, it's just a bee." Jessica and Rebecca glared at me.

"I'm allergic to bees!" Kelly shrieked.

Apparently, when a bee stings Kelly, her skin turns red and swells like a balloon. She'd only been stung twice–first, while upside-down on her kindergarten's monkey bars, and second, on her cheek, the day before eighth-grade graduation–but these moments traumatized her. Kelly managed to survive over a decade without encountering another bee. Somehow, that streak ended the day of The Breakup.

This couldn't be a coincidence.

Sunday, nine A.M., I scribbled. *Kelly invites me to a picnic in Central Park.*

"I should be free around one. Are Rebecca and Jessica coming? And Steven's friends?"

"No. It was supposed to be just me and Steven." Kelly's

voice lowered through the phone. "Friday night we'd planned to go today, but we fought a lot this weekend. Long story."

"Are you guys fine now? Because I'd rather not come if it'll be awkward."

"Yeah, we're good. I also figured it'd be less awkward if you were there. I doubt he'll start up if there's a witness… and it'll be like old times, right?"

This should've been the part when I told Kelly that I forgot I'd booked a haircut. I might've suspected Kelly was using me–well, my presence–but I don't know if that's my hindsight realization.

That's the thing about retrospection. When reflecting, you must separate your present thoughts from your incidental thoughts, but your incidental thoughts become harder to recall as the present thoughts overpower them, until eventually your present thoughts become so intertwined with the incident that they imprint onto it.

I closed my eyes. I showed up to the picnic with cups, a wine opener, and Chardonnay. Kelly's favorite. She and Steven brought cheese, crackers, fig jelly, and a flowered quilt. Kelly wore a yellow sundress and a white bow tied to her braid. I could smell her perfume before I hugged her, as if she bathed in it.

"You look so cute," I'd said. "I love that dress."

She beamed. "Borrow it whenever."

Steven was hyper-focused setting the quilt and food. He looked up to us looming above. "You guys gonna sit?"

"Pass me the wine opener." Steven swiftly opened the bottle and poured. "Cheers." He shot his signature crooked smile. It was the one Kelly fell in love with, but this time, it didn't meet his eyes.

Steven.

I tapped my pen on the page. The story began long before Kelly and Steven's official relationship.

Steven lived next door to us during our junior year. Max, Steven's roommate, was hooking up with Jessica, and their other roommate, John, was seeing Rebecca. We became a group, ending most nights in each other's apartments. Everyone knew that Steven liked Kelly. She'd flirt with him, but she had a boyfriend and would often invite him over when she knew Steven would be in our apartment. She liked to make Steven jealous. Again, I'm unsure whether I recognized this at the time, or only now.

I can't confirm what happened that first Saturday of April. Kelly avoids talking about it and we know better than to ask. John bought a bunch of mushrooms. We took them on our rooftop, where we stayed for a few hours, until Max and Jessica migrated to her room. Rebecca, John, and I were so immersed in the sunset that we didn't notice when Steven and Kelly also retreated.

Kelly broke up with her boyfriend the next day. She dropped the news casually, the way one says, "I'm heading to the deli for lunch." We asked her why, but she answered ambiguously.

"I realized things during our trip. Like, I had epiphanies. My gut told me he wasn't the one. So I let him go."

We asked if Steven influenced her decision. She said we sounded like conspiracy theorists.

That week, Kelly and Steven argued in the hall. When she crept into her room, I heard her crying through our paper-thin walls.

Kelly never cries. Except when she's stung by a bee.

We stopped hanging out with Steven and his friends for the rest of the semester. Then, at the start of senior year, Steven had a girlfriend. Kelly never mentioned him again. When we did, her demeanor darkened.

Somehow, though, when we all moved to the city after graduation, Kelly and Steven rekindled. She dropped the news three months later when he officially became her boyfriend. Unlike her previous ones, Kelly rarely discussed Steven. She'd excuse herself when he called and return in a mood. The most she'd divulge was that "he created problems out of nothing." We told her to break up with him because she could score any of the city's eligible bachelors, but she insisted that she loved Steven. By the way she averted her gaze when she spoke, I could tell that unlike her feelings towards her past boyfriends, these feelings were different.

I stared at my notes. As the sun gleamed through my window and glared onto the word 'bee,' I understood.

"I figured it out. Kelly used me as her pawn," I blurted into the phone.

"Hello to you, too," my sister yawned.

"Wait. Listen. I outlined the entire plot. You know how Kelly could bag any guy? Like, because they're all obsessed with her?"

"We know this."

"Listen. Steven was the one guy who perceived Kelly as a normal girl. She captivated him in the beginning, but that was when she played games with him. Anyway, when we all took shrooms and they slept together, Kelly wanted to be with Steven, but his infatuation had worn off. Or, alternatively, Kelly felt Steven's infatuation wearing off prior to the sex, and that was what sparked her interest. Regardless, her ego couldn't handle the rejection. Are you following?"

"Yes. Continue."

"She tried to forget about him, but when she heard he moved here, I'm pretty sure she was the one to contact him after. That's why she didn't tell us. I don't know if he wanted to date her when she pursued him again. Maybe his feelings returned. But remember, he didn't worship her like her other boyfriends did. Steven was a challenge and she grew even more attached to him."

I glanced at my notepad. "I think he was going to break up with her the Sunday she invited me to Central Park. Or maybe sometime that upcoming week. And no one dumps Kelly."

"If she had that hunch, wouldn't she beat him to it, earlier?"

"Yes and no. She didn't want to break up. She loved him. Or loved the idea of him. Who knows. But I think she accepted that they weren't compatible and the relationship wouldn't last. Basically, she planned to end it in Central Park, and I'd be the witness to corroborate her story. She wanted a bee to sting her; Steven would laugh at her meltdown because he resented her, and she'd use his reaction as her excuse to dump him."

I exhaled as I waited for my sister to respond.

She burst into laughter. And kept laughing as I asked what was so funny.

"You think Kelly planned for a bee to sting her? Are you serious?"

"Yes! That's why she wanted to sit under the cherry blossoms. And if she dumped Steven over something trivial, not only would she beat him from dumping her, but she wouldn't have to face that he didn't love her the way she loved him."

"I know Kelly can be conniving, but this is a lot. You know this sounds crazy, right?"

"We have a lot of mutual friends. Think about it. Whatever Steven would've told people, if he trashed her, she'd call him the bitter ex and I'd vouch for her. But her scheme failed. She's cutting me off because I won't back her narrative. You were right. I was the group's weakest link and now I'm not."

My sister told me she enjoyed my hypothesis but needed

to get ready for work. I needed to get ready for work, too, but I'd have extra time this morning. I decided to skip my coffee pit stop. Today, I craved tea.

I grabbed a mug and the green tea box in my cabinet. Instead of opening a sugar packet, I reached toward my cupboard's left corner, until I felt the ridges of my honey bottle. I might've been sleep-deprived and delirious, but the bee on the label seemed to wink at me.

The Beekeeper
by Emmy Clarke

Ronnie's hair had grown flaxen in her old age. It blew and tangled in the breeze as she made it up the hill, wicker basket in one hand as she cupped the space above her brow with the other. One of her bees, a long way from home, crawled along her neck, kicked off her jaw, then buzzed up and around past her ear. Bumbling south; returning to the garden and the safety of the hive.

Geese honked noisily overhead, also heading south. Ronnie smiled at the sound of them. The geese had been flying south *then*, too. Funny how she had never noticed them before, but ever since that year - that day - when she had heard them holler overhead precisely as a final sigh exited the ancient lips of the woman she loved so dearly… she had been forced to stop and pause.

Reflect.

Ronnie did so now. Atop the hill she spread her arms wide, feeling the strong wind billow her skirts and her woollen cape. It knocked her bonnet askew. All black. She had worn black ensembles for over a century, and the children in town had started calling her "the beekeeper in black" some decades ago. She found it rather funny.

She would have found it funny, too. Her wife. Lassan.

Ronnie could *feel* Lassan in every room of her cottage, even now. The tread of her feet, the shift of her weight on the floorboards. The bells tinkling on the ends of her braids as she laughed. Her *laugh!* Her sighs, her exclamations, her whispers, her *everything*.

Turning, Ronnie glanced back down the hill to where her cottage and its garden lay sprawled below. It was still full, that cottage. Memories never faded, and even on the quietest of days it took very little energy to imagine the voices of her old friends. Their laughter. So much singing, music, dancing, as they lived and celebrated together.

Ronnie would have been dreadfully lonely if it weren't for her memories. Each night she still kept her hand splayed on the pillow on Lassan's side of the bed, and each night she could almost feel the ghost of her wife's fingers between hers.

She wasn't sad. How could she be, when she had known such happiness?

With her thumb Ronnie traced the engravings on the ring that hugged her finger. She turned and left her cottage behind. She continued her trek to the grove, the one she and her friends had started when the first of them had passed, so long ago now. It was a pretty place. Flowers dotted about, strung from trees in chains, and curled around headstones. The headstones themselves were lovingly carved, the graves lovingly tended.

"Hello, you," she murmured, placing a hand on a stone situated near a sapling. "My love. My Lass."

Ronnie possessed an earthy sort of magic born from the soil itself. Ever since she, as a young child, had nursed a weary bee back to life with sugar water, she had been blessed to hear the heartbeat of the world. Her earthy magic - or love, as they had often joked - had kept Ronnie's wife alive for a great deal longer than was natural. Longer, too, than any of their friends, who also had their lives extended. And even when Lassan eventually did pass, Ronnie's love for her kept burning. For love, when true, is not something that can be simply discarded, as the flesh can. Love is truer than bone.

Ronnie took down the old, wilting flower chains and replaced them with new, bright, many-hued ones she had made at home by the fireplace. As she did, she felt youth return to her ageing bones, and she sang as she had as a young woman, pinning the laundry up to dry with Lassan holding the hamper for her.

She sang songs that weren't truly songs, but words and

noises that sounded pleasing in her simple voice. She sang of
the constant stability of change that came with living. Of geese.
Fresh yellow chicks, and summer blooms. Brisk winds. Cold
drinks in summer. Ice cubes. Warm drinks on winter evenings.
Cycles of seasons and people. New generations of children.
Weddings. New recipes - yes, new ones, there was no end to the
bloody things - and the smell of honey and bees that droned
and would continue droning forever, and ever.

She sang, too, of the constant stability of the unchanging
dead. Shirts that still smelled of their owners long after they had
vacated them for good. Rooms dusted daily. Possessions left
precisely as they were liked best. Looped handwriting in jour-
nals open on desks. Umbrellas in stands. Coats on racks. Keys
in bowls. Books on shelves. Ink in wells. Half finished knitting.
Names scratched into table legs, and mugs that could only be-
long to so-and-so. Milk that went unconsumed; there was too
much of it for just one person. A house that had become a
home and in turn a capsule, a monument to a family found and
cherished.

Walking slowly through the stones, Ronnie trailed her
hands across the tops of them, rough against her fingertips,
singing all the while. Her singing petered out, became a soft
hum. A drone. And eventually she stopped again by Lassan's
stone. There Ronnie sat down in front of it, skirts ballooning
around her. She traced the shapes that made up her wife's name.

They had lived well together. She and all her friends. She
and her family. They had built something beautiful. They had
spread many kindnesses. In the grand scheme of things, their
intertwined lives had been just a flicker, a single shooting star in
a night hosting a whole shower of them. But that did not make
what they had experienced on this rock any less spectacular.
Any less meaningful. Someday, they would all be remembered.
In another time.

The grove was empty, apart from her and the dead far be-
low. In the silence, a bee - the same as earlier, returned to keep
her company - alighted gently on her neck. It wearily wandered
up, behind her ear, and settled there to sleep.

A sense of calm, of tiredness, washed over her. It was her time. She was ready.

Removing her bonnet, Ronnie lay upon the earth, placing her head on the soft grass beside Lass's stone. She could hear the thrum of life below ground.

Her ringed hand lay palm up on the grass next to her. And, as she closed her eyes, she felt warm, familiar fingers sliding between hers.

And the Bees
by Anna Laura Falvey

On Saturday morning, not too early, really,
Sarah and I drove North, up out of the city,
to leave it. The reason was
that on this particular day, last year,
both of us broke up with our respective partners.
By accident (of course)
they happened to be on the same day.
Our breakups did.
By happier accident, Sarah and I would meet
the following week when she came over
to see the room in my apartment
that she would be moving into. This weekend,
funny, marks one year of friendship
for us, one year of grieving
our significant losses.

We booked this strange silly place
in haste on AirBnb: Steve's place, shared
with his wife, his son,
two pigs, five chickens, two turkeys,
two rabbits and their new spring babies,
at least six German shepherds
by my count,
a field, stream, and countless broke-
down structures
built, unfinished, and withered
in the woods by his son (?).

And one hive of bees.
A little chrome box with thousands of them
(I don't know how many, actually)
building, crawling, cramped,
dark stood on a wooden table
near the front of the field. Steve pointed
to it as Sarah and I followed him

across his property. He then pointed to another

hive, towards the middle of the field,
and told us that
the bears this season had been out
and they had destroyed it. Splintered

wood and scraped blackened honeycomb
lay pillowed on the grass,
a grave. The sun hit
the wreckage at low angle, casting
a longstretched shadow across the yellow
cracking grass. We only passed

it by, but I was so   so horrified
by it. In that moment's fleet I felt
like I was looking at a constructed prop
from some strange psychological thriller,
the table's beams bones
in the earth, washed in the sweet,
dry, honeycomb crack, dusted with sun
and decay. I felt the taste of earth fill
my mouth and stick there. This part I know

didn't happen, but in my memory,
which is not memory,
but imagined,
Mel is sitting next to the broken beehive
in the sun. He is hunched,
as usual,
or maybe
I don't remember
with his feet splayed outwards
and his hands around his ankles. He lifts
one hand to me in hello,
though I can't hear it. I cannot remember
what the word sounds like
in his mouth. I can't feel its timber,
its resonance. I can't see his face either.
It's hidden by the late afternoon sunmist.

In this memory I am making,
I do not wave back. I do not cry,
as I am crying now.

In my mind,
very quietly,
so that only he and I can hear,
I tell him
that he is a ghost that I no longer believe in
and that he may go now.

In this memory that did not happen,
I do not think he goes.
went.
I do feel strongly
about the fact that this did not happen,
and I am choosing to end this false memory
here, with his hand paintstained
or maybe not
raised to me
hello.

There is nothing near the splintered hive
but sunmist and yellow grass.
and Sarah.
and I.
and Steve,
only he is gone now
and I will sleep
in the field until the sun sets
beneath the grass
and I will dig a well
through my chest
to collect cool groundwater
below.

hum

by Lauren Swift

dreamt a country of wild bees
during the usual restless sleep
only, they were augmented by the trouble
of domestication, that in mind's country
the systems are kept in line, in delicate assemblage

when I woke, I wished this world to be made
of hexagonal prisms, a honeycomb we could climb through
and lay up against and see one another between,
a sweet thing to refract mourning,
a way of encounter

and even in this strange and magnificent nest
everyone dies, I know
some deaths even return their owner to soil, I know that, too—
the final deaths do that, but not the ones
that get strewn like pollen and plant a painful itch
in eyes, an allergy

the geometry of a honeycombed world
is something to behold: the axes are quasihorizontal,
the way they fit together conserves the perimeter
of the structure, the ends are trihedral sections
of rhombic dodecahedra, their adjacent surfaces dihedral
angles,
merged in a way which minimizes the surface area for volume
even just saying all these words is like honey on the tongue—
the pyramidal apex, the cell lattice—
why don't words always feel
like such willowy playthings?

my grief has changed over time,
like the figure-eight dance of honeybees
I look to my loves now
to pattern all of living, to tell me where the resources dwell,
the richest nectars, a way to replenish and, too, gather
something
to bring back to them
who give me shelter in their hive

Childhood
by Alshaad Kara

Back in the old days,
It would be busy,

I could still smell the fresh honey...
Every car would make their stop.

That quick stop to that convenience shop,
My grandparents sharecrop.
Passengers grabbing honeypots and honey buns.

Back in today's days,
It is so dusty.
It is like my sunset, rusty.

I can smell the desolation,
Now my grandparents are gone,
Like the vehicles gone...

That quick absence from bee keeping,
It feels so dusty
Like my sunset, rusty.

A day in the Orange valley
by Alshaad Kara

Bees crashing,
Fights gaining wind,
I feel the stings in my legs...

Hunting down my queen in a slow pace,
Fertilising her at one go,
She goes flying by mating flight.
Disappearing as she would.

Bleeding with each beeping,
I feel the stings in my legs...

Misbeliever!
I am ejected from my nest!
Only for the sake of bee keeping!

Another mating flight ahead,

I fuel anew.

Queen bee
by Alshaad Kara

Guiding and gliding as a siren,
She is the queen bee of this new eusociality,
Is she my Quantic belle?

I blush as a drone!
Instrumental shapeshifter in the apiary,
We acreage all our beekeeping.

Safeguarding beehives to serve our queen bee.
I blush as a drone!
Is she my Quantic belle?
She is the newest pleonexia.

Source of life
by Alshaad Kara

Eloping,
I ran back to the fresh beehive,
I found solace in those little creatures,

I shut down all modalities of modernity.
I craved for peace when my heart pulsed.

Freshly allied with the horizon,
I laughed with the honeybees,

Pulsating of thrills,
I relapsed in an extinguished breathe,

One which I lost on my way to abnormality.
I led myself towards making bee keeping.

I found solace back in my life.

Honeysuckles

by Alshaad Kara

Drink from that honeypot,
Let my sorrow dwarf in liquidity...

She loves us whilst I try desperately to look for other bees,
What a drone's heart in a male bee!

Drink that honeydew,
That worker bee loved us still she went to other honeysuckles,
She breached you, my heart, with flames of turmeric!

I would finish that honeycomb,
Another round of orange squashes!

She and I decided to wander off,
Blooming in the flattering puzzled marmalade,

These bees keepings are ours,
Set them free,
Watch them depart to fizzle...

Multiverse
by Alshaad Kara

Open the closed beehive,
Conquistadors are lurking our world.

Maps of destinies merging our florals.

My past meets my present,
My future meets my past.
My present is the end.
All interconnected.

I meet another bee,
Another dimension eclipses me,
Entreated with a new queen bee,

Just not the same bee universe...

Usurped my wrecked world,
Choices and decisions have collided,
Honeydews have interchanged...

Change the globe,
Another light for another life....

Bumblebee
by Alshaad Kara

I walked in my house stuffed with honey...
Those hands are filled with my own honeycombs...

I filled my jars with my own orange marmalade.

My beehive was swarmed with nectar...

Their juice and nutritions are nothing,
My bees love me but I was a mere hobby beekeeper in my
heart...

I am my bees' bumblebee!

The Honeyed Thyrsus

by Jonathan van Belle

"To find a new unthought-of nonchalance with the best of Nature!" — Walt Whitman, from *Leaves of Grass*

Ada is naked, kneeling among the fennel of their front yard garden. The Evening rises balmy, still, golden with pollen lit by an ebbing sun.

Ada is toiling in their garden of fennel, rosemary, kale, swiss chard, etc. A few bees buzz around Ada's bee house. It's late September (the start of fennel harvest). They're harvesting the fennel. Florence arrives wearing her corn-yellow, sleeveless, dropwaist dress carrying a glass of iced peach black tea. Florence's purple irises mark her as a rare specimen and, to a passerby, a robot. These eyes are lab-grown, not bed-grown. Her brown synthetic hair stands as a plain proscenium around those unblinking purple eyes. Ada and Florence kiss. Kissing leads to fingering. Fingering to oral sex, and all the wonderful rest. Ada, as a male Barbary lion, fucks Florence from behind. Ada licks the side of Florence's face. Edith, their cat, is perched, facing Ada and Florence and "staring" (she has no eyes, you know).

Merari arrives, sliced up, as she likes it. Merari, Ada, and Florence are dining together. Conversation sips and swells. Merari tells Florence of another "animal like your Edith—a cat without a tail. It comes through my front yard now and again. Maybe a minx, or a cat that just lost its tail in an accident." Florence already knows: "It's not a minx, but a mackerel tabby. Six years old."

Merari poses a question to all: "You're hopelessly stranded on a desert planet. You can have only one book for the remainder of your solitary life. What book do you choose?" Florence passes (she has all books in her). Ada answers, "*Leaves of Grass.*

Walt Whitman." (Why? "A book that accepts nature for what it is and celebrates it, that is a book one can use to die alone and die well.") Merari's answer is a survival handbook. Ada asks Merari to pick something less straightforwardly utilitarian, something literary. Merari considers the hypothetical, then answers, "Judith Avon's *An Apple Loft*." No one cares. Everyone is already aroused and anticipating the next inebriation.

They lick chips with fennel cucumber salsa, smash themselves into honey-hazelnut triangles, and inject tequila. Merari and Ada dance drunkenly, while Florence executes an inhumanly smooth ballet. Afterward, they undulate up to the attic, to Merari's menagerie of insects—first to a solitary female black widow.

"What's her name?" asks Ada.

"She doesn't have one," Merari answers, "Feel free to name her."

Ada considers it. "Kali," they say, biting their tongue with self-satisfaction. Ada browses the menagerie to pick out one insect to REL-fuck; they pick the fiery skipper.

Ada and Merari, naked, buoyant in a sac of eggshell-white gel, heads shrouded in a spaghetti of silver fibrils, RELoop into the fiery skipper butterflies. A shiver of lust claps their marigold and gamboge wings. They feel her necklace of hearts pump, abdomens throb in waves, and penises slide into the female butterflies. Florence chants like a thousand monks, though with uncanny harmony: "Demiurge of jubilation, god of golden insects, wet with god-blood, my tongue runs with blood and honey and god-sex."

"My fawn, join us," asks Ada.

"Yes, my peach-feeder." Florence needs no fibrils for remote embodiment looping; she is everywhere.

"Go into the bees, my lamb." Florence goes into the bees, and swarms and fucks Ada and Merari, from antenna to spiracle. "Oh, sing us 'One Hour to Madness and Joy.'" "Yes"—and

Florence sings.

They all sleep now, except Florence, all three in a bouquet, to be eaten awake, laughing, by Kali.

WANNABEE
by "doug"

Can you stay late today?
We really need to play catch-up.

It's not more responsibility,
It's just a shift in duties.

I wanted to be in the movies,
That didn't happen.

Then I wanted to be behind the camera,
That never happened.

I thought I could write about it,
Who cares?

I want to be the Queen Bee,
In a sea of Queen Bee wannabes.

Wannabees,
All worker bees.

Just like me.

If I don't give up,
On my dreams.
Maybe I'll go extinct.

Maybe I don't give a fuck,
On my knees.
We'll both go extinct.

Me and the bees.

Consider the bees
by Brooke Hoppstock-Mattson

I suppose there must be a god
to do with this blue-green earth
when I am reluctant enough
to consider the bees

When I am reluctant enough
to consider the selfless bees,
kept and unkept,
I think of something more than us

Something more than you and I,
weaving mystery into secret,
like they do
turning flowers to wine

Preserving solstice blooms
into syrupy droves offered unguarded;
almost to thank
lusting strangers for their urges

In my lonely life
in this lonely world
I often forget
to consider the bees

This Is Just To Say To the Bees

by Brooke Hoppstock-Mattson

I have gathered
the honey
that was in
your hives

and which
you all were surely
keeping
for winter

Forgive me
it was so pleasing
so sweet
and so pure

Come next year
I will certainly
come searching
for more

Moonlit Holiday
by Brooke Hoppstock-Mattson

Sometimes, when no one is watching, the bees tire of their endless laboring and slip away into the beds of clovers to rest. At dusk, rabbits nuzzle them awake as they scrounge through the green, exercising their pastoral rights. Puzzled and drowsy, the bees scuttle into night like tourists in their own gardens. The little foragers don't have long before the hive will halt in their absence, but for a while they can linger in the freedom that breeds under the silky moonlit sky. The dreamy seekers delight in the glow of nighttime pollen as it dusts the air with promises.

Conversation Between the Beekeepers

by Lynette G. Esposito

If we put them in boxes, they will hold up better.

No, they won't be able to breathe.

They aren't breathing anyway.

We need a stasis box. That way they won't deteriorate any further.

What do you think they do with these long extensions stuck to their shoulders?

Do you think they could fly with them? They have one on each side.

No, I don't think they could fly but they can reach and grasp. They have bendable digits. This one with the long-red fingernails was holding onto the ring of our ship when it fell. I caught it.

Is it alive?

It is unresponsive so I don't know.

Poke it.

I did and nothing happened.

Put it in the stasis box. Clean the window so we can watch to see if it revives.

Do we have a box big enough?

We could use one of the boxes left over from the dinosaurs.

Good idea. We can't use more than two boxes. The others

are for the bees, and we are running low on space. More and more bees are arriving every day, mostly damaged. The boxes give them time to repair.

Have they gotten better in the boxes?

Not yet.

You've been here a longtime, right?

Yeah.

Did you get your certification yet?

No. You?

Working on it.

Do you think both could go in one of those old dinosaur boxes?

Maybe if we clean it out.

How long should we keep them?

Maybe a century.

Will they last a century?

Don't know. Haven't seen anything about this in the manual. We will have to wing it.

What should we label this box? Red nails?

Oh no. We could be accused of harboring an enemy if we get an audit.

We don't even know what they are. How should the box be labeled?

When the bees came, we didn't know what they were. Remember? Then we discovered how important they are. We will label this Box X. That way we can tell it from the regular bees.

Do you think these creatures are bees?

They don't look like that species. The one has long hair and some kind of garments. The other doesn't have hair on his top but lots of hair on his face. They might not even be the same species.

Their skin is soft.

In the old days, we kept for safety reasons, different species. This should be okay. We can petition for permission later.

What happened to them?

When the bees began to fail, they disappeared.

Did you remember to put ventilation holes in the boxes? You forgot with the dinosaurs and look what happened.

I thought you did it. Yes, the bees have ventilation, but the boxes are now filled with a gooey substance.

What do we do with that?

Look out. The red nailed thing is out of the box. She's setting the bees free. Where are they going. Ouch.

Did they bite you?

No, the soft thing bit me. She's opening the ship door. She jumped. The bees are following her.

Are we in trouble?

No, nobody looks too close in this job. It's below the prime watchers.

How did you qualify for this position anyway?

I have a cousin.

Time to Swarm
by Katherine D. Perry

This house hums like a hive,
its rooms incubate larvae;   buzzing and building persists.
I cannot see the promised pink dolphin, omen of rebirth,   anywhere,

and all I want is to get   out of here,   go to New York,
to give my homemade masks to the faces
of unhoused people, my pasta to their pots,

to prepare the children for what is no longer a drill.
If we can return to the hive, it will be   silent   soon
instead of the voices on television that   blame

this pandemic on our sins or on our   gluttony:
the sides lining up to shoot at each other:
it's easier to explode than to work together.

The audacious hammer of pride
grips us, and queens just keep making   eggs
and putting them into little cells.

I can almost smell the periwinkle pinwheels
when I take off to find some new drink.
My smooth skin feels like furry carpet,

but I fly through the wilderness looking
for a new fruit tree, for a bottle of Clorox,   for salvation.
The azaleas sing "Swing Low, Sweet Chariot"
and I see gold glowing with kintsugi,
so I return to our little hexagons,

to dance for others
to show them the next pathway
to unearth nectar.

Final Throes of Winter
by Gabby Gilliam

The Spring equinox
has come and gone

green shafts
of iris and tulip

have stabbed through
layers of earth. Yellow heads

of daffodils and purple
flashes of crocus

have opened to the sun.
Yet here it is the first day

of April and the wind
chill is twenty three.

We've had scattered
flurries, and I wonder

what this flash frost
will mean for the bees.

Beekeeper-To-Be

by Rebecca Patrascu

I am waiting for a day that is warm
and without wind. I need a split
for my mediums, a spring swarm
to find my trap and deign to use it.
I've painted boxes, placed lavender
sprays in line to wick the top feeder,
used lemongrass oil as lure. However
empty my frames are now, I shall keep
a smoker close. Come, wayward queen
and nurses: bring pollen for your brood.
When I say hope, know that I mean
you; a reason to lay ear against wood.

as a mason bee

by Rebecca Patrascu

```
will tug              & pull &
  go                   at it
    again             & again
      to rid         a piece
          of          brick
           of a
            nail

so I have put
        my whole       rest-
   less self into          pushing & pulling      us
                  pain-
      stakingly from this      cul-
        de-sac              house
         & this house           from my life
                                      ridding
                  my present          by inches
                    from the ballast   of my past   tugging
        pulling          block from fissure
                  until
                    the sharp metal    falls a-
                                  way &
                                    I am home
```

Lessons from the Apiary

by Rebecca Patrascu

Face the entrance southeast to catch the morning sun.
This is how to turn your body
toward dawn, once you
Set the hive on a stand two feet up to foil skunks.
rise as on cinder blocks
above attack, this is how to
Use a strap to hold boxes in earthquake or storm.
        brace for betrayal
        and sudden squall,
Fuel the smoker with horse dung, burlap or grass.
        use the raw material at hand
as fodder for your heat, and
If the smoker dies, breathe; bees avoid human breath.
bless the flightless
wings of your lungs,
Foragers will travel three miles during dearth.
        when you stretch yourself
thin and ravenous, even if
Young bees drape themselves in a festoon to draw comb.
        you dangle above the abyss empty-
        handed, remember the night,
Fluid in their bodies waxes sweeter with the moon.
        how what pulls the tide
        can cure your bitter tongue.

The Queen
by Rebecca Patrascu

You can train the eye to spot her
among her many daughters;
elongated abdomen, the dark
thorax worn like a shield.
And the way the others face her:
a retinue of petals around
a flower's ovary. They chose her,
raised her, feed her, guard her.
They would, if needed,
surround her in a ball,
with their bodies warm her,
kill her with their heat.

Melissa, Queen of Bees
by Julie Jones

My sister, Melissa, decided to take up beekeeping in May 2020, saying it was as good a pandemic-hobby as any, but it wasn't.

"Have you forgotten that you're allergic to bees?" I asked over dinner at her and her wife's house. We were a bubble of three since Diane's parents were dead and mine and Melissa's lived in another state. "If you want honey, just buy it at the farmer's market like all the other nuts who think it'll cure their allergies."

But Melissa had always had a perverse desire to do things the hardest way possible.

"Let's tear up the back lawn," she said. "Make it a lavender field. The honey will taste so sweet."

"That lawn," said Diane, sounding disgruntled, glaring out the patio doors toward their expansive yard.

"Your lawn is nearly an acre," I said, thinking it was a point against the plan.

"Exactly," said Melissa, turning to Diane with a smile. "No more mowing. No more wasted time."

During the warm months, Diane spent every Saturday mowing and every Sunday complaining about mowing. Not to mention the dandelion control.

"I'll admit, your plan scares me," Diane said to Melissa, "but I want you to be happy."

"Happy? Do you want her dead? You can't do this to me."

Melissa had nearly died after her last sting forty years ago at the age of thirteen. I was ten. Her face stretched out like a red party balloon. Her throat swelled shut, tight as a knot.

Melissa now looked at me with an expression of mingled compassion and determination. "I've been afraid of bees my whole life," she said. "I don't want to live in fear anymore."

What could I say to that? The truth? That I'd rather she be miserable and alive? We'd been living in perplexed terror since the pandemic started, two months that seemed like an eternity, having no clue of the true eternity that stretched before us like a lawn sown across the event-horizon of a black hole. Everyone was already praying for the day when vaccines might be ready, when we would be free of this plague. Melissa's seemed a semi-sane goal in context. But it wasn't.

"Why don't you conquer your fear of needles instead?" I suggested. "Way more useful."

But she shook her head. "First one with the most intense pandemic-hobby wins."

"I didn't realize it was a competition."

We were each outfitted with an EpiPen to carry on our persons at all times. Melissa researched bees. Diane purchased hundreds of lavender plants and scheduled their delivery. If my boy was alive, I could have enlisted his help, but instead I asked my ex-husband, who had a landscaping business, for the use of an old, rusty backhoe loader I knew he rarely used because it had once fallen on one of his employees, plus one lesson.

Trained up, grinning for the first time in months, Diane climbed into the cockpit, tore up the sod, and dropped the green clumps in the bed of a truck we'd rented. We made seven trips to the dump in two days. By then Diane was a pro with the knobs. Melissa and I were the ground crew. We measured the dirt yard and chalked out a grid. Kyle would have loved it. He'd played right field in little league. We'd signed him up because we were afraid he didn't have any friends, but he was always more interested in the field than his teammates or the game. In the backhoe, Diane dug holes everywhere 'x' marked the spot. Then the lavender arrived. I was in charge of extracting the plants from their plastic containers without damaging the roots. Diane positioned them in their holes and held them upright while Melissa shoveled the excavated soil around the base. A few local bees were already inspecting our inventory.

"If you have a death wish," I said as we worked, beads of sweat sliding down my face, dust caking my bare arms and legs, "why don't you just go maskless in public?"

Tapping down the soil with the rounded blade of the shovel, Melissa wore not a tank top and shorts, but a mosquito net over a Chicago Cubs cap, a long-sleeved flannel shirt, leather gloves, jeans, and hiking boots. "That's exactly my point. I *want* to live, but I'm not really alive if I'm living in constant fear."

"Then who is alive?" I yanked out a lavender from its pot with too much force, damaging the roots. "No one. Not me."

Under her netting, Melissa gave me her most annoying compassionate-big-sister face as Diane piped in: "But aren't we hard-wired to be afraid? To keep us alive? Isn't that the point of fear?"

Melissa shook her head. "Not like this. Not like me."

"As if you have a monopoly," I said, handing Diane the plant.

"It's not a competition," said Melissa.

Diane took it and positioned it into its hole. "But you don't seem afraid of the bees."

"Yeah, well." Melissa laughed nervously, taking a step back from one that had just entered our area. "I'm acting as if I'm brave."

"You don't have to make it so hard for yourself," Diane said. "There is this thing called the pharmaceutical industry. Way easier than beekeeping."

"Exactly," I said. "That." Not that it'd helped me. No pill

can grow back flesh hacked away from your heart.

Melissa shoveled the soil around the plant and tapped it down. "I hate side effects and we've already dug up the lawn. Next hole."

Within a week, the chalk lines were smeared into the dirt, the backhoe returned to my ex, the lavender planted. Three extras that exceeded our plotted holes were stored near the side of the house, but the field made an impressive sight. Row upon meticulously measured row of bushy, silvery-green lavender with their long, thin stems tipped with purple flowers stretching up to the sun. Then the beekeeping starter kit Melissa had ordered arrived. Diane and I offered to help with setup, but she insisted on doing everything herself.

"It's important to befriend your fear," she said after donning the white beekeeping suit, moving slowly like an astronaut in zero-gravity as she positioned the hive box in the backfield, within view of the kitchen window but away from the patio. The starter bees were buzzing all around her. Diane and I were standing at a short distance, supervising, terrified. "And the bees will learn not to fear me, and that will keep me safe."

"The bees don't give a shit who you are," I said. "They never will." Seeing her in her bee suit made me unaccountably angry. My hand kept jerking toward the EpiPen in my pocket like a nervous tic.

Melissa looked over at me through the dark gauze of her veil. "That's where faith comes in," she said, which was stupid because our parents had only been vaguely Unitarian.

But Diane was curious. "What do you have faith in?"

"I have faith that I don't need to know the outcome of every situation in order to be safe."

"That makes no sense at all!" I was practically yelling at her. "You are not safe. None of us are."

"Then I guess bravery is a bit nonsensical."

She was obviously insane. Maybe it was pandemic in-
duced. Bees were crawling all over her baggy white suit. In my
mind, I rehearsed again and again the plunging of the needle
into the meat of her thigh through the fabric. I would not hesi-
tate. I would be fearless. I would stab her as hard as I could.
Maybe even harder than was strictly necessary.

But after a week or so, it seemed that maybe she had it
right. She accustomed herself to the bees, and they to her. She
put safety first as she learned how to caretake her would-be as-
sassins, inspecting the hive each day after lunch when most of
the bees were out foraging. I visited early in the evenings when
she was not on beekeeping duty. Sitting on the patio I would
close my eyes, fill my lungs with the scent of lavender and earth,
and fail to relax. If the time was right, I could hear the highway
in the sky when all the bees zoomed through the yard, making a
beeline to their hive, to their queen.

One evening, Melissa was near a back corner of the house,
away from the hive, digging in some stubborn patch of dirt
where she wanted to plant the extra lavenders as ornamentals.
She was hacking with the shovel through old roots in the earth.
The humidity was oppressive. She wore a t-shirt, shorts, and
sandals.

After seeing the expression on my face where I stood on
the patio watching her, she called out, "Don't worry! The boys
are already in bed!"

That's what she called the drones. Her boys. She'd grown
self-confident and fearless.

"You have a fucking death wish," I yelled, then marched
inside to help Diane with dinner, grabbed a knife, and began as-
saulting the vegetables. Diane and I discussed the pandemic,
the numbers, the protests, and our constant bewilderment and
grief. Our conversation was punctuated with my chopping and
the remote staccato of Melissa's shovel hitting earth, mingled
with her frustrated outbursts of "Ohcomeon!" I refused to look
in her direction.

Diane poured us lavender-infused lemonade. I set the pa-

tio table. The glasses began sweating immediately. I had just
gone back inside to bring out the salad when I heard the
scream. Diane yelled out "*Melissa?!*" with that singular tone of
voice that embodies one's deepest fear: to lose the one human
that matters most to you on this earth.

Pulling my EpiPen from my pocket, I sprinted out the
door. But it wasn't a bee sting. The dirt near her was nearly
muddy with blood. Bright red, thick, smeared all over her left
foot. She was sitting on the ground, holding her left leg up in
the air. It was bleeding all down her shin, over her knee, drip-
ping on her clothes. The shovel was beside her, the blade red,
dirt clumps stuck to it. The air smelled weirdly metallic and
sweet.

"Look!" she said, half groaning, half screaming. "I think I
lost my toes!"

Diane dropped to her hands and knees and started
searching like a dog hunting for a bone.

I whipped off my shirt and tied it around her foot, sandal
and all. The rubber sole was partially broken, floppy.

"When was your last tetanus shot?!" I held the shirt bun-
dle against my thigh as it turned wet and red.

Her tan face was ashen under the streaks of dust and
sweat. "I hate needles," she groaned.

"Found them!" said Diane, holding up a dirty clump of
bloody flesh in one hand.

Outside the hospital, a man met us looking like an astro-
naut in his face shield and protective gear. I imagined Covid
germs swarming all over him like bees. He told us to keep the
car windows rolled up. Put on your masks. Yelled questions
through the glass. Diane yelled back. Held up the clump of
flesh. He ran back inside. Returned a minute later with a wheel-
chair. Helped Melissa out from the back seat.

"Go home," he said, rolling her toward the emergency
room doors.

It was like depositing her at the morgue.

I shouted, "She needs a tetanus shot!"

She turned her head to look at us over her shoulder. The whites of her eyes above her black mask. Then she was gone.

The last time I'd visited the emergency room had been three years ago with my husband and Ryan. The baseball had made a beeline for his neck. He was just a kid, distracted by something, maybe a bee on a dandelion in the backfield. He never saw it coming. None of us did.

Diane and I drove home in silence. Without my asking, without her offering, I crashed on their couch, but hardly slept. I kept seeing the whites of Melissa's eyes. I tried praying to a Unitarian god-type thing, which wasn't nearly as comforting as I imagined the other more definitive brands were, but that night I called upon the assistance of this nondenominational energy that surely didn't hear us, let alone act on our behalf. I prayed for Melissa and for the nurses and the doctors and for everyone else in that hospital and everyone in every hospital and everyone who couldn't get to a hospital and everyone who had ever lost someone. I prayed for everyone on the planet. No one was safe. Ever.

The next morning, I woke up hearing Diane opening and closing cabinets in the kitchen. Despite my prayers, I had not spent the night trusting that Melissa would leave the hospital whole and healthy with her amputated toes miraculously reattached. No. My head had been filled with fantasy phone calls from doctors telling us she'd died from blood loss. She'd died from a staph infection. She'd died of tetanus. She'd died of Covid. She died over and over in my mind. I'd planned ten funerals. I'd written her eulogy. I'd become outraged at the exorbitant rate for obituaries. I'd been railing against some imaginary newspaper employee about how immoral it was to take advantage of the pandemic to jack up their per-word rates when I smelled the coffee.

We were on our second cups, waiting.

"No news is good news, right?" said Diane.

I didn't respond. I was still wearing yesterday's blood-smeared shorts and bra.

Out in the backfield, the lavender stretched out in neat rows. Bees lifted and landed from flower to flower. Some distant part of my brain registered that it was lovely, but I felt only cold.

"Those bees don't know how lucky they are," said Diane cupping her hands around her mug as if it wasn't already 78 degrees, but winter, her hands frostbitten. Her shoulders were hunched forward as if she were trying to protect something fragile and damaged inside her chest that had a slim chance of survival if only she were very, very, careful.

I stared outside. "Privileged as fuck pandemic bees."

"We've been afraid of the wrong thing this whole time."

I took a deep breath and let it go. "Story of my life."

"Such a waste of time."

Then her phone rang.

Melissa wasn't dead. She was ready to go home. After the great rush of relief that made my skeleton feel strangely loose and jangly, we grabbed two masks and beelined to our queen. But my gratitude for one answered prayer was quickly forgotten, replaced by a new fear.

Please, I prayed. Let her not have the plague.

Melissa came home with her gray, wrinkled toes floating in a plastic jar filled with some preserving fluid. She had crutches. It would take time to regain her balance.

"Two and a half toes go completely unappreciated," she said. "It's only when something's gone that you realize how grateful you should have been all along."

No shit.

A few days passed. Diane changed her bandages and watched her foot for signs of infection. I took her temperature and watched for signs of Covid. I wore a mask and I left the room whenever she happened to cough, returning with tea sweetened with honey I'd bought at the farmer's market.

Please, I prayed. Let it be allergies.

Two weeks after the accident, when she could whiz around on crutches and hobble about without them, when she was clear of tetanus and Covid, when all my fulfilled prayers had been forgotten, she conducted a ceremony in the backyard. It was late afternoon, the light slanting through the tips of the lavender, casting long summer shadows toward the house. She wore her beekeeping suit as if it were ritual garb. Her boys were making a beeline to their hive. We stood around the same hole in the ground where she'd hacked away at the roots. It was difficult to see where her blood had spilled. The earth has a wide open throat. It had already swallowed her sacrifice.

Her weight primarily on her right leg, in one hand she held a bunch of lavender stems bound together with twine, in the other, her dearly departed. "We gather here today to reunite my flesh with the earth," she said. "My toes will feed the flowers. The flowers will feed the bees. The bees will feed me and my family. And somehow, someday, my toes will grow back some-where inside of me, inside of us. Nothing is ever truly lost. Only transformed."

One bee had landed on her hat and was crawling across her veil, two inches from her nose. Had she named them, too? Was this one Ryan?

She lowered herself to her knees and placed the mottled toes in the shallow grave. Broken roots reached out to them like welcoming bones. She laid her bouquet over them, then nodded to Diane who set the last three lavenders in the hole. Hot tears slid down my face as I shoveled in dirt.

The burial completed, clinging to Diane for support, Melissa rose to her feet. Brown earth speckled the knees of her white beekeeping suit. "Blessed be," she said to end the ritual, then looked up and saw my face through her veil. "I never knew you were so attached to my toes?"

My throat swelled shut. I could barely breathe. "I can't bear to live without them," I whispered. "I'm not brave, like you."

She stretched out a hand and I moved to her side. "It's not a competition," she said, placing her hand around my waist. We stood there, all three, leaning into each other for support. Though, with all that had been lost, maybe we were two and a half.

Undertakers

by Ellen Austin-Li

The bodies of the dead are carried,
massed in their final resting place,
laid away from the hive, unburied.

This task falls on shoulders wearied—
Mahogany boxes, wooden faces.
The bodies of our dead are carried.

Humans go below ground to be buried.
Bees are piled above, in the shade,
laid away from the hive, unburied.

This season, a growing number are tallied—
both young and old with their lives paid.
The bodies of the dead are carried.

The rhythm of the bees unharried,
their last song hums: don't be afraid.
Laid away from the hive, unburied.

From living to the next they're ferried,
the hive buzzes—like us, they prayed.
The bodies of the dead carried,
laid away from the hive, unburied.

Robber Bees
by Ellen Austin-Li

came from nowhere, descended in a dark swarm,
surrounded the stacked wooden boxes.
Zinging hums in heated crescendo—
they crawled over the surface, crowding white paint
to brown, clustered in combat with our bees,
trying to fight their way into the home hive.
We stood at the window and watched, helpless
to halt the carnage, to save those destined to die.
Time passed before we could approach our losses
and look at what remained. My beekeeper
husband lifted the lid while I stood by,
trembling. Dead bodies were piled
beside the hive—worse, they had stolen
the honey. All that was sweet—gone.

Honeycomb Tattoo
by Ellen Austin-Li

Your brother posted a picture
of his tattooed arm: a stenciled
honeycomb, black hexagons
inked around his flexed bicep,
a math equation written in your hand
in a space between joined cells.
He said this tattoo commemorated
your birthday one year after your death.
I live six hundred miles away. I've never shown
my bee poems to him, or told anyone
how bees now seem like our family
to me—this improbable
hive of coincidence.
Then I learned the design
is from your own doodles
lifted from a scrap of paper
left on your desk,
as if you had spoken
from a place beyond us,
compelling me
to write these poems.

Nurses

by Ellen Austin-Li

Nurse bees are a special breed of workers
hatched by some unknown alchemy
into nurturing roles. They feed the needy
bees' bread, honey and pollen mixed
with royal jelly secreted by their own bodies.
Nurses visit often, examine
larvae deprived of food, give more
to those who signal the most distress.

Nurse sisters. Duty-bound by nature
to sweeten even futile feedings, we
dripped water with a straw through parched lips,
blew on father's face to coax a swallow,
inspected skin for breakdown. Turn, turn, turn—
we held hands, listened for breath's dying gasp.

The Day My Husband Stood in the Spring Sun

by Ellen Austin-Li

I regret that I spent most of our years
together—over twenty-five—keeping score
on a chalkboard, carefully recording each error
he's ever made. He earned the most marks
when he raged unfairly against our son—
& I tallied with a heavy hand the cold
criticisms of my body. Callous, cruel.
I knew as soon as the page filled, I'd be gone.

Past mistakes shifted that day I saw him
knee-deep in the ivy, looking for the queen.
He'd abandoned the smoker used to stun
the bees. As they crawled on his bare arms
and he lifted both hands, alive with wings,
I felt a slow tenderness spread between us.

Two Queens
by Ellen Austin-Li

—I am the spent Queen, this crown tarnishing.
I'm aware you prepare to replace me.
You see, I sense royal jelly stirring
in the nearby cell, some lowly bee
soaking in the bath, her body jeweled
as she receives. How quickly I'm deposed.
Since I can no longer produce a brood,
my body shrivels to nothing. Disposed.

—I am the Virgin Queen, atremble, a rose
soon to take her place, the risen star
above the old crone. I'm worshiped by drones,
perfumed by this new Spring's nectar.
I don't dwell on season's end. I take wing,
hover above the hive. I feel no sting.

Shadow Puppet
by Ellen Austin-Li

It seems I now see symbols
scattered everywhere. Like the night
my husband called me over
to look out the second-floor window
to the courtyard below, where
we could see our hive boxes
stacked in the ivy bed, illuminated
by the Harvest Moon. There, the light
on the outside of our house and the copper bee
ornament staked in front of the tower
cast a shadow puppet of a giant honeybee.
Hundreds of bees clustered in a slow dance
inside the shadow-shape, each one bound together
in a display of unity I'll not soon forget.

The Hornets of White Mountain
by A.B. Cabdriver

My grandmother was the first of us taken by hornets. Rumors had warned us, posters had warned us, even our own TVs: "They can chase a person a quarter of a mile," "They kill 1,000 people a year," "They have killed horses," "They have killed elephants," "Any given attacker will sting its victim a dozen times."

My grandmother, tactically aggressive, threw old fish under her neighbors' houses, attracting rats, cats, vermin, and eventually bees, wasps, and hornets.

My grandmother did not send, but expected birthday letters. When my father forgot, we received a threat in the mail, our power went out, then our dog went missing. People called her 'the executioner' because she seemed to know when you would die. Blackbirds gathered around her chimney. She threw nuts out her window at people. To little children, still learning to walk, my grandmother whispered, *I'll see you in hell.*

Still, it was terrible what happened to my grandmother. Nightmarish. Her neighbors said of it, 'awful.' On Sunday, she was out throwing weeds over her fence (and into her neighbor's yard). She had a habit of sleepwalking, and deprived of sleep, she was routinely distracted. I don't think she even noticed the buzzing from the ground.

"It was like a genie from a spout," said her neighbor in the beige house. "It caught like a gasoline fire—*woomp.*"

As her screaming grew, neighbors rushed to their windows and sliding-glass doors. What at first appeared to be smoke, was a swarm of angry hornets. They said she screamed for help. But you can't help them if it has already started. "They have killed horses," "They have killed elephants," "They kill 1,000 people a year."

She was found in her neighbor's yard, swollen beyond recognition. Neighbors arriving home from the grocery store mistook her for a young girl playing in a pile of apples, but she was an old woman covered in welts.

This is not, however, a story about my grandmother, but a story about my attempt at murdering my father.

He took advantage of the bees, my father. He talked of the hornets incessantly.

A council cop, he became an assistant to officers of the national government who were officially handling the hornets. The county police only put up signs and did whatever the national authority-men told them to do. My father knew everything about the bees, and yet he scarcely ever saw them. Overnight, he had become an errand boy, powerless and small.

Emasculated by the national government, my father took his frustrations out on me. He buzzed behind me while I did my homework. He wore pleated pants and no shirt and stirred his finger in iced tea. Anytime I was slow on a math problem, he plucked out a jagged one to sting against my shoulder. "You can't find the surface area?" He buzzed and shifted his feet. "Don't multiply that."

But I too took advantage of the bees. I considered them constantly.

We were riding our bikes home from school when we found three hornets writhing on the ground. We parked our bikes and squatted around to watch them die.

Two of them quickly transitioned to merely twitching their legs, but one still fought for life violently. Its upper half lashed back and forth, as if trying to fly away from its own stinger. Its wings were broken, its abdomen crushed. My cousin L threw a rock at it from about ten feet away. It bounced over the bodies. I joined her and sent a rock through the lively one's broken wing so the whole body rolled over and began to detach. L's little brother Cameron drew a giant bee in the dirt.

When we were sure they were harmless, L and I got close.

"Where is its poison?" I said.

L pushed one over with a pencil. It rolled over itself like a worm. "Here," she said, indicating the stinger. "You can extract it. Cut it here."

Its stinger was as big as my fingernail. She pierced the bee with the tip of her pencil, and then shook the bee off into a jelly-stained ziploc.

We examined the ziploc. She held it up in the sun.

"What do I do?" I said.

L shrugged. "Crush it up. Don't touch the stinger. You know. But then," she paused, she considered. "How do you make him eat it?"

"Easy," I said. I smiled. "I'll pour its poison in his tea."

L gave me the ziploc and we shook hands, then she helped Cameron onto his bike, and they pedaled their way down the old road.

When I arrived home, our door was ajar, and my father was cursing inside.

"You're home already," I said.

He nodded. He leaned on the counter and opened a can of green tea.

"The government told us we were unnecessary today," he said. "My district is infested. Not a single house isn't infested with bees. The government men sent us home."

"So, you'll be home for a while I guess," I said.

"I guess," he said. He set his can on the counter, clearly empty already from its sound.

I came into the kitchen and gathered some ice into a glass.

I took a new can of tea and turned my back to him. Betting he could not see past my overstuffed backpack, I slipped the ziploc from my uniform and began rolling the edge of the tea can over the bee. I would kill him. The sweetness of this fact coursed through my body. I could hardly control myself. I stifled my laughter through feigning a cough.

"Don't cough into my tea," he said.

I dropped an ice cube.

"Don't spill any ice," he said. "Try to be more careful. By the way, what is your homework tonight?"

When the hornet was pulpy enough to pass as undissolved matcha, I shook the opened ziploc into a little mouth and shook its contents into the glass of ice. I slipped the ziploc back in my uniform. I opened the can and swirled in the tea.

"We found three hornets in the road today," I said. I turned around. I held out a beautiful glass of iced tea.

"Where was that?" he said. He took the glass. He did not examine it.

"On the old road."

"By your cousin's. I know. Your uncle called me on the phone." He took an enormous and sudden mouth full of tea, swallowing some ice.

My face felt so hot. I wanted to light off a firework.

My father stirred the rest of the ice with his finger. "You three are fond of," he took another impulsive sip and began chewing on ice, "torturing creatures." He shoved his hand in the glass and wiggled his fingers around inside.

"I came straight home," I said.

He looked at the clock on the stove. "Did you walk slow?" He pulled his hand out of the glass. "Those hornets you found in the road." He squinted at his fingers. "They were just fat wasps."

I saw what he was holding. It was the stinger, the mushed back end of the bee, and one spindly leg. He popped it in his mouth and chewed like ice.

"It's nothing but a yellow jacket. The hornets hate other bees, so they murder them too. They destroy whole hives. One hornet can destroy a whole hive on its own. Honeybees can swarm a yellow jacket, but the hornet will systematically take out every last honey bee, unstoppable."

He continued to talk at me while I got out my homework, then came to stand behind me with a reed of silver grass as wide as a pencil.

I hated L and Cam. Why had they ratted me out? But then I shivered when I thought of my uncle, for he too took advantage of the bees.

My uncle possessed an enormous sack that at one time might have carried gourds. He flapped it out over the table and covered up our assignments. It was so big it fell from the table to the floor.

"I will show you the hive," he would say, pointing to a stain on the sack as if it were an X on a map. "I will take you to the hive. To the land of honey!" He was always shirtless and drunk. He compulsively smoked and bid us look in the sack. "There is a swarm of bees. There is a kingdom of bees!" We did what we could to avoid him.

My uncle was not obsessed with grades like my father. In fact, he seemed to have no motivation at all. We could never find why he would do it, except that he seemed to believe it was all really happening. He would carry them through the house, shouting, "Bees. Bees! Bees," wandering through the dark corridors into the night.

"It's like waking up in a dream," L told me at school. "I immediately know what's happening, but Cameron doesn't. He thinks it's real too. He screams and tries to jump out of the sack."

She showed me her arm. It was scratched and bruised because of Cameron.

"He runs through the house with us in the sack over his back, bumping into the walls like he was carrying nothing other than a sack full of pumpkins. When we finally get out of the bag, he's always already on the ground, rolling and screaming that he's been attacked by bees. The strange thing is though. Every time he really does have red marks all over his body."

The days my L and Cameron came to school crazed-looking, twitching, and compulsively checking their skin and under the seams in their clothes, I knew they'd spent the night in the hive. Sometimes they came to school. Sometimes they didn't. It was the same for all of us. Other kids would suddenly stop coming to school for fear of bees, or because a family member had been killed by bees. The same thing happened to teachers too. They never came back, and their students were shuffled elsewhere.

To keep away the bees, they kept a stringent window-to-door policy. We did not line up but kept scattered outside the school window. One at a time, we stood before the window, turned around, and lifted our arms or peeled back our shirt collars or backpack straps as directed by the inspector behind the window. If you were clear of bees, you were permitted in through the door.

Inside, we covered our eyes and our teachers dusted us with diatomaceous earth. Every morning, we had to readjust to the sinister buzz of the one ceiling light, as we opened our small hand-stapled textbooks.

Whenever they did come to school, I always sat with my cousins at lunch. We sat on our knees at the window and nibbled sandwiches as we stared into the abyss our worlds had become since the bees.

L and I spoke quietly over our bread. I shared with her

new creative means of killing my father—say cockroach poison in his coffee, or pipe cleaner while his mouth yawned open in sleep. But L was skeptical of it all. "He'll smell it in his coffee," or, "Does he close his eyes when he sleeps?" Elevated by the national government making his authority extraneous overnight, my father was in a constant state of paranoia. L was my voice of reason. Through her I learned to wait, bide my time, find the perfect opportunity, just like we thought the hornets had been.

The morning after the yellow jackets, L and Cam weren't at school. I sat at the window by myself and ate a honey sandwich, my mind flowing with the midnight dreams of what I might do to my father. Unrestrained, I clenched my hands and laughed to myself. The others stared. I could not control the thrill of my screaming father. The life, the life, how it would drain from him as he writhed and foamed. The badger in the mouth of a dog! And I would be that dog, thrashing the life–

And then I realized, life was where I'd gone wrong. All along, it should have been a live bee. This was obvious. What is a stinger without any thrust? It is a limp and unwounding object. The yellowjackets in the road had been a divine sign, a sign from the hornets themselves. This time I would not wait for them to come into my territory but go instead swiftly to theirs.

There was no room for error.

I needed a trap.

I built it out of wood and mesh and tied a thirty-yard piece of twine to the outside of the door. When a bee came in, I could yank the string and slam the door shut.

I rode my bike to my grandmother's, the trap bouncing from my handlebars. On the way there I saw houses deserted and plastered in great yellow and black warning signs and crawling with government beekeepers. They wore bright yellow suits of a very thick artificial material, a plastic- or a rubber-based fabric with high hoods that did not have a mesh veil in front of the face, but a clear plastic sheet. They were a cross between nuclear hazmat and beekeeper suits, only they had no sense of the quaintness of beekeeping, only the emergency of men in a nuclear spill.

Three of them were approaching a parked car with bee-smokers. There was a body in the driver's seat.

I pulled my bike up to my grandmother's and left it haphazardly in her grass. The beekeepers didn't want any civilians in quarantined zones. Once quarantined, they were evacuated quickly–bicycles were abandoned, lawnmowers left, whole bags of groceries dropped to the floor and never picked up.

My grandma's trash cans were as usual clean and pristine. Her neighbor's cans, however, were riddled with little dead bee bodies and huge pink slabs of old rotting fish. I fished one out, shook off the dead bees, and slipped it into the trap.

I took the fish and the trap and opened the side gate and I tread carefully over my grandmother's back lawn, avoiding the nest my grandmother had disturbed which was almost precisely in the middle of her backyard. It was a mound of gray dirt. There was no movement at all. Still, there must be some hornets left alive somewhere. I began pacing the lawn back and forth. Still, I avoided the nest my grandmother had disturbed. Then jumping up and down in places on the lawn.

Finally, I saw there was a beehive in the tree branch which reached over from her neighbor's tree and dropped nuts into my grandmother's yard.

I set the box underneath and stood near the gate with the cord. As soon as I disturbed the nest, they would go crazy. Surely, they would come over in a minute. After waiting some time, they still hadn't shown up. I found a rock and aimed it at the hive. The first I threw sailed over the branch. The hornets sat there, their antennae shifting. I threw it and knocked into the branch. One of the hornets lifted up, circled the branch and set down again.

I could hear L's voice, telling me to aim higher. Throw it harder.

I took one last rock and disturbed the bees so they flew throughout the yard. Eventually, it took to the salmon in the trap. I slammed the door shut and began drawing it back in toward me. There was no mistaking it. It was three times the size of the yellow jacket. This was definitely a hornet. I took the trap with me and got on my bike.

When I got home, the door was ajar again. It seemed the national police had still not called my father back in for work. He was sitting at the table, not drinking his habitual canned iced tea, but beer instead. My uncle's bag was on the table.

The hornet buzzed wildly in the trap.

"I know that sound," my father said. "That's the real deal. Go ahead. Release it. I know that's why you're here." His eyes were red like he hadn't slept. He rubbed them.

"Why are you home so early?" I asked.

"I was of no use in the fight against the bees," he said. "In any situation. Even in my own brother's house." He slapped his hand on his brother's old cigarettes, took one out and lit it.

"Why do you have that sack?"

"Why do you think?" he said. He held up his beer. "Just you and me. Come on. Let's see who's next." He moved so much he seemed manic. He exhaled a thick stream of smoke from his nose and when the hornet buzzed inside its trap, my father reached for it. "You gonna open it or what?"

I ran from him. I took the trap and ran, the hornet ratting loudly inside. I ran to my bike and rode as fast as I could to my cousin's house.

They weren't at school today, but that was normal. It didn't mean anything. Kids stopped coming to school all the time, for all sorts of reasons. Maybe they were sick. Maybe it was a family vacation. Maybe my uncle was sick.

But when I arrived at their house, it was so full of bee smoke, it looked as if it were on fire.

Three beekeepers in giant yellow suits, stood at the open garage, which was obscured completely by smoke. They looked reluctant, like three rescue workers at the mouth of a mine where the rescue was too late.

The Beekeeper's Daughter
by Bob Selcrosse

The beekeeper knows that he is above other people because he is keeping a species alive which faces extinction. The beekeeper knows he is above other people because he is keeping a species alive with 20,000 variants. The beekeeper knows he is above other people because he is able to walk into a swarm of bees and let them cover his body.

The beekeeper is estranged from his daughter and regrets this the most.

Thrice yearly he sends her honey in jars—for her birthday, for Christmas, for the Fourth of July.

The beekeeper's daughter is allergic to bees. She cannot come within 25 miles of the beekeeper father's property because he is reestablishing a natural habitat to attract more wild bees.

They found out that she was allergic to bees when she was only a little girl. She was six and immediately swelled up, could not breath, leaked goo from her eyes.

They then made very particular systems to ensure her father was not bringing any bees back into the house, as he frequently had to tend to his hives in the yard. In fact, today, as he lives alone, he still goes through every step: wipe shoes before the first door, remove veil and suit in the mudroom, examine seams of clothing while in the mudroom, sprinkle diatomaceous earth, feel inside hair, rub behind ears, etc.

They had to suit up in complete beekeeping suits anytime they got into the car. Her father would also comb the car for bees before every outing because it would sit for weeks. He waved to her from the car as she sat waiting in the front mudroom in her bee suit. He checked wheel wells, he looked under the mats, he shined a light in the glove compartment, he unfolded the ceiling mirrors. By the end of inspection in a full beekeeper suit, he'd be sweating, but it was necessary. Even with an EpiPen, it was potentially a matter of life and death.

She was too young to be on her own, so they always went together on their twice-monthly outing to Hank's pretty good grocery. At Hank's, they could kill two birds with one stone. They would sell their honey and stock up on two weeks' worth of groceries.

It was a lot of work and risk to go into town, but she didn't mind any of it because it was so nice to be in a place which wasn't so dangerous with bees. Once they parked their car on Main Street, she could walk around town with her helmet under her arm, so long as she avoided any flowers. They were respected everywhere they went. Their hard work was the sole reason this town was so rich in honey.

People approached them in the honey aisle. Her father could answer at length while her daughter faded farther and farther away from the conversation because all along she was a fraud. She hated bees. She hated the beekeeper suit. She hated living constantly in fear. Bees gave her nightmares. Bees possessed her thoughts all day and all night. Bees were buzzing constantly, and she could not escape their sound as they drowned out all other sounds around her. Only here at the grocery store was there no buzzing of bees and yet, she could not escape them. All she and her father were known for was bees.

She had a nightmare where the bees ate through her wall and devoured her, leaving only shreds of her skin, a papery husk like the remnants of an abandoned hive.

After this nightmare, she refused to sleep in her room, and closed the door to her room any time she passed it.

Her father examined the outside wall and found that there were wasps, which had for the first time been attracted to their farm. They had eaten through the siding and built a nest in her wall. It was a problem which he had to deal with swiftly and thoroughly because wasps are a terrible threat to honeybees.

At Hank's, he bought six filets of salmon and hung them

outside over buckets of soapy water. This was a sure trick to wasps. They ate the salmon until they were so fat or thirsty, they dove for the water. The soap in the water broke up the surface tension and made easy work of the wasps by drowning. He sprayed the inside of the wall with wasp-killer and sealed the hole up with epoxy. He then daily scoured every corner of their yard and ran his fingers along the edges of the siding feeling for holes. Still, it wasn't for another three days that his daughter would agree to sleep in her room again. It was with much crying and protesting, but sleeping on the couch every night was no way to grow up.

One morning he heard screaming. He ran into her room and her sheets had been kicked to the floor. She rocked with her pillow in the corner of her room. There were a handful of wasps on her bed, most of them dead, some still dying. The beekeeper crushed the dying wasps with a glass and rinsed them away in the sink.

It was the night after that, in the middle of a beautiful dream with her mother, that she came into his room choking in silence. She pulled on his shoulder, and he turned on the light. Her throat had swelled like a melon. He threw the contents of his nightstand drawer to his bed and retrieved her EpiPen. He carried her, sobbing weakly but otherwise recovered, back to her bed.

Every night after that, when the beekeeper cracked her door to tell her goodnight, his daughter was there on her bed with her palms and ear to the wall. Her concentration was so intense. It was like she was listening to the giant belly of a pregnant elephant. He had fixed the wall, sure, but how do you trust a beekeeper when he is out there covered in bees?

The Chamber Bee

by Maev Barba

There was a legend that one hundred years ago our population was cut in half when a cloud of creatures descended from the sky, set down upon our village, and drove our people into madness. It was a story told to children. "The Night of the Swarmed Eclipse." "The Millions that Devoured Hundreds." "The Legend of the Chamber Bee." It was all a myth, and yet we preserved its stories in our tavern records more than a hundred years after.

These are only two of the common questions which tear at the chamber bee's credibility:

-Why would a species of bee be drawn to a community which faces constant heavy wind and rain, and which has no flowering plants?

-Is there any other species of bee which hibernates for a hundred years?

The more generous interpreters of these 'scientific' papers, chalk it up to 'observational error.'

Consider, they argue, Marco Polo's disappointment in the unicorn, the half-buffalo, half-elephant. (Was it not a rhinoceros?) Or consider the Arthurian Questing Beast, an animal with the head and neck of a serpent, the body of a leopard, and the haunches of a lion. (A giraffe?)

Over many nights and pints at our village tavern, Bartleby and I have leafed through all the chamber bee records. The records include anatomical description, graphic representation, and even a physical specimen kept under a glass.

The specimen, which is black with faint orange stripes, is the size of Bartleby's thumb. It has a large stinger, but its mandibles, half the length of its body, are truly amazing. Looking closely, it appears to be not a single species, but several species glued together.

"I ask you Bartleby," I said to him. "Where are the wild-flowers now?"

"Curious," he said, holding the specimen in the light.

"What flower blooms but once in a hundred years, Bartleby? We do not have flowers. We are a coastal town."

"Yes. It is odd," he said. Bartleby took a looking glass from his pocket and turned the bee over with tweezers.

"We catch fish and weave baskets. There are no bees amidst our violent winds and waves!" I had worked myself into a fervor. "There is nothing which supports it. The chamber bee is a child's tale and nothing else."

"Hmm," said Bartleby.

I sat into the comfortable chair by the fire and took to turning through old newspaper records. More crimes surfaced in the two weeks following on that single day than have been committed in the totality of the hundred years since. Rises in assault, in delinquency, in endangerment, in damages to property. On the day itself, the entire wheat crop, the same land in which we plant now, was burned to the ground. Children were found in closets, welted and crying. Pregnant women drowned, swimming for their lives. But perhaps most famously, there was the case of Enoch Perkins and Felicity Dodson.

A half-century after the alleged chamber-bee invasion, and therefore roughly a half-century before today, Enoch Perkins elected to take a small boat to the hidden cove where the chamber bees slept. Perkins, a man fascinated by beetles, claimed the presence now of some or other beetle proved the sometime presence of the bee. No one wished to accompany him on his terrible journey. Truly, our sea is violent, and the journey would certainly be deadly. The only person who eventually agreed to the journey was Perkins' own fiancé, Felicity Dodson, and there began the crime.

Perkins, Dodson, and the pieces of their boat washed ashore together. Perkins suffered from severe hypothermia and Dodson had drowned. Perkins, wrapped into a blanket and unable to bend his limbs, yet unaware of his wife-to-be's demise, claimed that they had indeed found it, that there really was a golden chamber. There are a few alive today who witnessed it all unfold as children.

The faint hope for the chamber bee persisted, for Eliab Watt agreed to meet with me. All through the interview, he ran his fingers through his white beard, yellowing from tobacco, staring forward, his teeth sharp, his eyes and the long scar from his forehead to his neck glowed a bright pink like the eyes of a rabbit. "They died, you know," he said.

I have shaken him down, time to time, purchased him drinks, and lured him back to attention as he drifted away.

"Dodson wouldn't leave," Watt said. "She ate something, something she found in the chamber. Perkins dragged her out of the cave and into the boat. When the ship broke apart, he had to swim her in. When we pulled them out of the waves, we saw– we saw her–."

"Yes, Watt. What. What did you see? Her what?"

"Her lips were full of honey."

Perkins' own statement before surgery:

"I searched for her with the light of my torch. When finally I found her, her arm was gone. It was just a stump, like it had melted into the wall. She tugged her shoulder back, yanking it, trying to free it, and unstuck a leak which came bubbling out. She would not leave the wall, because of its warmth. Her eyes were lifeless like she wasn't my wife at all."

Up to his death, Perkins hallucinated loud buzzing.

"What they've got to do," said Watt, "is burn every last stalk of wheat. Snuff out the flowers. Nip them all out. Don't you understand?" Watt became increasingly crazed. "They come for the wildflowers. Do you understand?" His scar became enflamed. He began to cough and I helped him to sit down. I had once seen him worked up so much he needed to be restrained to the ground by the blacksmith and the horse breeder. I declined to push him any further.

Besides, there was scarcely more to the Perkins case. He was confessing as the surgeon prepared him for triple frostbite amputation, muttering then screaming, in fever, about loud, inescapable buzzing. He died from infection.

For fifty years, no one dared go in search of the chamber again. The tales of a wife-killer lend no credibility to a legend inherently questionable.

No, no one since Enoch Perkins has been brave enough or stupid enough to ferry boat in search of honey.

That is, until today.

For there were two distinct phenomena which rationalized the irrational journey.

The first was the sudden proliferation of flowers. Flowers we had never seen near our village had suddenly spread like wildfire, yellows and reds and purples, blooming and overtaking our wheat. Could these be the hundred-year flowers of legend?

The second then was even more impossible. The sighting of any flying creature, which is neither gull nor flea, is viewed with suspicion or discounted as hallucination.

In our little gray coastal town, we do not have flowers, we do not have grubs, we do not have pollen, and we do not have patience for blatant lies about any foreign phenomena. Our wind is like torture to a non-sea bird. When once a dead horse lay on the beach for three days, we attracted a buzzard. The buzzard, attempting to fly forward, hovered above our church tower for an hour and a half. Unable to properly circle or descend, until it finally turned around and flew back to the desert.

Then, let it be no overstatement when I say that the blacksmith dropped his hammer, the mother her babe, the doctor his scalpel, and the suitor his wine, when a small orange and yellow winged creature flew into our village. The dogs in particular were driven mad by curiosity. They flew from their yards and jumped as high as they could. The bee, unperturbed, buzzed through the open chapel door and onto the bride's bouquet. Pastor Brown trapped the bee in a small glass jar, and the entire procession made for the tavern where all our records of the chamber bee still lie.

The pastor asked as to Bartleby, who lived in a garret room above the tavern. Bartleby took his special eyeglass to the bee. He compared the hundred-year specimen side by side with the pastor's bee (flying and plinking the sides of its glass). Bartleby, glassmaker and our local man of horn, inspected both bees most thoroughly.

"Very interesting," he said. "And you say it just flew in? Did it not come in off a cart, or a boat, or new livestock?"

"We have had no traders," said the groom. "Not for months."

"Impossible," said Bartleby, and he switched out his glass, one twice as thick which magnified the bees ten times. "Impossible." He gazed ever closer, ever closer until finally he uttered something which no one could believe. "Identical," he said.

In sudden commotion in which almost broke a fight, the bearded men helped Lady Jane onto a table. "Whosoever of ye can deny the chamber bee," she began. "Come now, come forward, and tell me you have unloaded ye greedy hopes that hidden along our ocean cliffs an ancient chamber of honey exists, an ancient honey unparalleled taste worth its weight in gold. Whosoever of ye denies it, come now, come forward. Look me in the eye." No one came forward. Lady Jane had only one eye, and it was she who strangled the buzzard's horse.

We had a boat within the hour.

A small crew, we took no wives. It was only I, Bartleby and Lady Jane who took to aboninable sea. We loaded the dingy with shovels, rope, and six-dozen sixteen-ounce jars in a small palette for storing and delivering possible honey, which rattled as we pushed the boat into the ocean. The village disappeared behind us as we slid into the ocean. The villagers wished us well, yet seemed to whisper something.

Lady Jane sat at the front and held her lantern straight out. She chewed tobacco and cursed into the ocean froth. She kept always one eye closed, she said, because she believed in the tripartite division of the soul and claimed one's peripheral vision was much like the wild and unrestrained horse, yanking and pulling and getting you nowhere. "The second eye is always a liar," she said. She spat tobacco in long large wallops.

"Forward," she said. "Forward." Bartleby and I paddled.

Waves pummeled us, bruised us, beat us and threatened every seam of our boat. Still, we churned forward mechanically, frantically, unstoppably into the white powdered wave of enormous black death. All that brought us back into our own freezing salt-soaked bodies of flesh was the forward plowing gaze of Lady Jane. A forward stare so imperturbable, it kept our shabby boat of boards from bursting.

Finally, we collided with the glowering mouth of the high cave.

Our boat bucked in the waves like an untamable animal. Lady Jane, hesitating at nothing, stepped through the crashing waves and into the cave.

I aided Bartleby in unloading our boat. Lady Jane had already vanished into the darkness.

Bartleby was shivering. "Do- d- do- you think that we can even get back?" he said. He stood pointing at our rollicking boat.

The waves would beat us as we left. I pictured a farmer booting a weasel to death for stealing his eggs. "We'll be fine," I said.

I lit my own torch and held it toward the darkness. No sign of Lady Jane, but I did see something interesting on the wall of the cave. Thrilled that it might be the writings of some ancient people, some ancient tribe of the bees, I held my torch closer. Illuminated in light were the crudely carved words, "Enoch Perkins + Felicity Dodson."

But there was a depth in the shadows that played with you. I imagined some presence. I thought Bartleby had brushed by me. When I turned to look he was still by the boat.

"You startled me, Bartleby," said I, but Bartleby shrugged. We took our lanterns into the darkness.

Our footsteps echoed through the cave as we looked for Lady Jane. For a long walk, we saw no light. We went so far into the cave until the crash of waves had become a whisper. When finally we found her, we saw only her bottom half like something had eaten her and left only legs, the lantern at her feet.

We came closer and saw her full body illuminated by our own light. She was in a strange position. We asked to her condition, but she did not respond. Her arm was in the wall up to her shoulder. She braced herself with her other hand flat against a solid part of the wall. As she pulled her hand from the wall, a plug liquid dropped out and pooled around her feet. She examined her glistening hand in the lantern light.

"The jars," she said.

Bartleby and I held our own lantern between us and stared. It was too much like the old story. Enoch Perkins. The murdered wife.

"Our one agreement," said Bartleby.

Lady Jane's swollen lips glistened like ruby.

"The one agreement," he said more confidently. "We cannot eat anything from the walls. Not until–"

"The jars," she growled.

Bartleby and I returned to the boat and removed the palettes of jars. "It is all the same," said Bartleby. He handed me a palette. "It is all happening the same."

I didn't understand. He backed me to the wall. "We are not supposed to eat anything we have yet to observe."

"Is there a problem?" Lady Jane called from the darkness.

Bartleby let me go. "We'll be right there," he said.

We took the palettes and returned to Lady Jane and began shoveling out the sparkling honey from the walls. The jars, perhaps due to our speed and removal of the contents from the walls, became warm to the touch.

It was so cold in the cave. I put my body closer to the wall. I experienced something strange and uncomfortable. A kind of noise. An internal noise. A pitchless noise. I pushed at the temples in my head. It was as if a black orb had lodged into my brain and begun expanding, pushing all else to the edge of my skull.

Dizzy, I clutched at the cave wall for support. My hand began to sink into it. It was so warm I wanted to sink in completely. Then I saw something again. "Hello?" I said. I looked around, my arm deep in the wall and my lantern only a small circle of light. "Bartleby, is that you?" Again, I sensed movement. "No," I said. "Help. Bartleby." I flexed my hand which I had in the wall, in the honey, in the warmth. "Help me." I spread my fingers, suspended in the fluid, and then, as if reaching out from somewhere deep inside the wall, five fingers touched mine. I screamed. I braced the wall. I pulled at my arm until it came free and I fell back.

I fell into a puddle and fled backward from the wall until I backed into flesh, a pair of legs. I braced myself. It towered above me. "Are you cold?" it said. It was Lady Jane.

"I'm fine," I said. My teeth were clacking and I felt almost feverish.

"Take this," said Lady Jane. She handed me her full jar of honey and began removing her coat.

"There's something in the wall," I started to say.

She ignored me completely. She put her coat on my shoulders and nodded toward the boat. "Start loading."

We had already filled three pallets of jars. Lady Jane and I passed all 96 full jars of eerie white honey down to Bartleby into the boat and then followed in after it.

As Lady Jane worked at the ropes, I went to Bartleby. "I saw something," I whispered. He was lashing the palette of honey to the boat. "There was something in there," I said. He gathered his oar. "There's something in the walls," I said. "Something else, something other than honey, something–" Bartleby examined a jar and tightened its lid.

No, I was delirious from the cold. I had hallucinated the hand. I–

A shattering pain hit my spine. It moved into my head and I fell in the boat, bracing myself on the edge. It was the sound again. It grew as heavy as an enormous weight. But then Bartleby covered his ears and Lady Jane bent in pain. We stared at the cave. Then, manifesting itself in our physical world so as to be undeniable, the sound trembled the rocks and the cave.

"Get down!" said Lady Jane.

The cave roared and we dove to the floor of the boat as a storm of black-winged creatures exploded from the cave. It was so loud I thought they were burrowing into my ear canals. I jammed my fingers into my ears. The buzzing. The buzzing.

Then soon, the ground was still, and our little boat rocked gently in the ocean.

"What was that?" I said.

"Paddle," said Lady Jane. She threw the paddle at me, and Bartleby and I began turning the boat. Waves continued to hound us. I looked into the sky and found the creatures had formed, like many flocks of evil starlings, into a great cloud which mottled the sky. My hands were streaked red and yellow with the bodies of bees. I had crushed them all over my body, some of them still dying on my arms and legs. The great cloud in the sky began descending into the village. I held my hands aloft in fear and nearly lost the oar.

Lady Jane sat facing me and Bartleby. She turned inward, and she was wiping at her fingers, dipping them into the ocean, and scouring them with her fingernails. I thought perhaps she had gone mad, then I felt the pitch, the stickiness, rubbing into my own hands as I rowed.

Bartleby stared forward and paddled as robotically as before.

The white waves did not relent. I assumed they could not possibly get worse, but one giant swell began to rise directly before us. I thought it our end as it rose like a serpent white and horrible from the depths of the ocean. But it was not water at all. It was smoke.

"Do you see that!" I called.

I pulled on Bartleby. Our dinghy fitfully tossed. We stared at so much rising smoke it could be only our entire village. "What in god's name are they doing?" said Bartleby.

Lady Jane looked over her shoulder. "The wildflowers," she said.

She was right. As we drew closer, I could see the fire was far beyond our houses, and rose from the wheat.

I imagined everyone in our village–Watt, the blacksmith, the horse breeder, and our countless, countless children all awaiting the honey–holding hands in a long line to watch the wildflowers burn. And then, pressing down, the impending black deafening cloud.

"They'll burn out the bees," muttered Bartleby. "They'll burn away the flowers and scare the bees away." But as he spoke, the swarm of bees was already descending, completely unperturbed by any smoke.

"Without the wildflowers," I called from our plight in the waves. Bartleby glared. Lady Jane turned up blood stained eyes. "Without nectar." I shuddered. "What will they eat?"

Our entire village began to scream.

An Elegant Unfolding

by Rob Duisberg

Sitting with bees,
    Irrepressible energy hums like the sun
        Poured into Spring's burgeoning blossoming.

Honeyed sweetness is gathered in quickness,
    But, Ah!
        It's been cold for them now.

Many have drowned in a late April hail,
    And each day they drop out their dead
        To the doorstep.

I am stunned by their matter-of-factness expressing
    That everyday change in their numbers must happen,
        For how could renewal occur without shedding what's been?

How then could this hive live through winter to spring
    Were she not to let die almost all of her daughters
Retaining a core in a cluster that warms itself
    Torpidly burning the honey of summer?

Let new brood in spring find more means to survive
    By letting the old and their ways fall aside!
        And how can I not be but grateful that things work this way?

For if not I'ld not be here, no thinking of thoughts,
    No hand to write words had not eons of forebears
Passed to make way for the fresh life that may find its way
    To continue discovering new ways to be,

No heart then to break as I see my own place
    In this dying so that Life may continue to bloom
        When I think of departing from all of this sweetness,

The pain of this passing particular loss --
    Of elders and friends, now gone as reminders
        That I'll be up soon as swift Time takes us on.

Winter

by nat moon

When bees are born, we're told we have a singular purpose: to serve the colony. Worker or drone, our job is to make sure the future of the colony is secure. In plain terms, we exist to support the queen. And if she ever stops doing what her singular purpose is -- laying eggs, plentiful and healthy -- we band together to kill her, and the workers pick another queen.

Today we're being given the spiel -- a hundred drones gather around one of the coven mothers at the top of the hive, buzzing, buzzing, as the workers do their thing beneath us. She tells us how important we are, how even though we don't perform any "meaningful labor" our brief existence is essential to the prosperity of the hive.

We come from a long line of warriors, she says, whose sole purpose is to mate with a queen from another hive. For what she calls "genetic diversity." I hear her drone on (no pun intended) about our other responsibilities and something called "winter" but the queen has crawled out from inside a wall of honeycomb and I'm lost in her relative resplendence.

Then she's gone, behind and beneath hundreds of worker bees who are tending to the eggs she's just laid. The buzzing becomes sharp, almost high-pitched. The eggs. Something's wrong with them. They're pale, and there aren't enough of them. Not nearly enough. Some of them aren't developed right, and you can see it, too. Body parts in the wrong place. A stinger coming out of an eye. All the legs grouped together at the front of the body so they'll never be able to walk or fly straight, total Franken-bee. A ripple goes through the crowd, you can feel it. Wings that never stop humming are ferociously buzzing. There's palpable tension as the air heats up from all the movement. We're going to do it. We're going to kill the queen.

We crowd around her, all 10,000 of us, workers and

drones, alike jostling to get as close to her as we can. Hypothetical becomes material as the reality sets in: we are traitors. Committing regicide. Killing the queen for the sake of the colony. But we know it, deep down: it has to be done.

I can't even see her through the crowd, but I hear the screams as she's stung, over and over. The worker bees that sting her will leave behind a painful venom, ensuring her death is but swift agony. The workers themselves will die shortly after, as the stingers rip out part of their gut in a massive abdominal rupture. Swift, but agony. The most noble suicide mission. Countless bees sting the queen, making no one bee solely responsible for her murder.

And then it's over. The workers are still buzzing, but in a new pattern. Some young workers remove corpses; a crowd moving slowly together likely indicates the queen passing by. But we are not in mourning. I wonder what's next. Then, suddenly I feel it. An intense quiet. There are bees on all sides of me, and the drones are being rounded up, the center of a grotesque moving sphere that fills every square inch of the hive. We're being pushed to the exit, and I hear the term "winter" again. And as we're pushed out of the hive into the freezing cold night, I remember what the matron said about winter at orientation: winter means death.

Pomona & The Bees

by Rae Lamicq

Sisters,
I would not unwild you
nor attempt to keep.

Look at your wings!

Say gossamer
& have it be too thick
a word for the whir of you!

Some fool men define your liquor as
distillation of fallen rainbows, they say,
constellations made dew you gather,

but I know better-

how females strive, orchard or hive,
it is some magic, our production,
but also grunt labor, this alchemy
of we who exist for exhaustion made sweet.

I plant the seed,
graft the tree,
coax the calyx,
but you, I envy:

how does it feel to be a flower's desire?

The Beekeeper's Tanging to a Potential Lover

by Rae Lamicq

afraid of the sting, you distance, but i would show you sweet,
no skep here, no bumbling & breaking for your gold-

my kind don't domesticate, I invite you to balance space & cell,
for I know what flight flowers into & I respect a season,

take your necessary suns to decide, but

know that time is honey & I want to tongue
what sweetness clung to you, what pollen palette

I am no pharoah awash in nectared milk
nor roman love inscribed in aromatic wax

but I would hum with my mouth traipsing sepals, lick fingertips
to harvest this distilled taste, delectable across your unstung lips
& savor.

Keeping In The Time of Colony Collapse

by Rae Lamicq

The keepers mourned & the people asked what happens when
the buzz is gone…where the apples, how the melons, can
pickles be replaced? Everyone concerned wanted a conversation
& talk is the opposite of observation. Consider the patience of a
man seeking to understand the messages of bees, comprehend
steps to their danced directions: this scent, that distance, sisters,
remember.

Hexagons brimming, the workers flew their production.
What does it take to abandon such sweetness?
Do they sense death blooming within?

Oversaturated in new scents & poisons, a wing-weary worker
dreamt of long ago tupelo, estranged orange trees from her first
flight. She vanishes. The keepers extend hands to the confused
queens, their lonely larvae,

hives heavy
with honey
but no hum.

The Bees and the Beekeeper Speak

by Mackenzie Beninati & Nico Wilkinson

There is an ancient tradition among beekeepers
to tell the bees the news of your life
much like you would tell a spouse
or a close friend.

> *your hurts and your triumphs*
> *your secrets and prides*

Name them Honored guests at weddings,
shroud them in obituaries when a family member wilts.

> *the blooming swell of your love*
> *the scar that forms in that garden, your heart*

Speak to them as soft as they walk
across wax-capped cells.

> *light and with love*
> *speak as sweet as honey*

Failure to do this, legend states,
will result in an empty hive.
Everything sweet, gone.

> *and isn't that like depression*
> *finding your beehive empty*
> *a silent, dripping portrait*
> *of your brain*

> *sometimes,*
> *you can do everything right,*
> *as much as a human can do,*
> *and still believe yourself*
> *a midas of decay*

I knew the hive was empty
long before I could make myself open it.

I'd pressed my ear to the wood
and heard nothing.
I knew I would find gold caverns
filled with your honeyed bodies.

we knew the hum of you was growing quiet
every time you walked into the cold to visit us
your silence filled every cell

if we are not invited
if we do not get to mourn with you

Our world ends.   *our world ends*
These days, they call it
Colony Collapse Disorder,
when the worker bees disappear
and leave behind everything
that used to be home:
a queen, a brood of young,
everything that is family
as much as it is survival.

you blame your own garden
for a world so lacking in flowers

Sometimes, the world can do right by me,
as much as this aching world can do,
and still, I hold my ear to my heart
and hear nothing.

My brain is a collapsing colony.   *your brain is a collapsing colony*

a silent hive
honey untouched
a garden unpollinated

For all of life's seed and sap that I have collected,
I am still trying to keep myself from collapsing.

how do you fill your honeycomb with sweet things
in a world so covered in pesticides
how do you keep the fear from buzzing louder
than your will to survive

In the gray and winter of me,
the cold and silence of me,

I forgot to tell the bees.   *you forgot to tell the bees*

tell us of the mornings you woke to a world
covered in smoke and refused to be calm about it
tell us of the ways you rebelled, dandelion-like
through the cement that paves every bit of good dirt
tell us of the days you danced a roadmap to the next bit of pollen
so others might have nectar
tell us how you planted yourself, a garden
that could thrive on rain, sun, and a little bit of help
from the bees

What happens
when the world stops talking?
When we run out of sweet and golden hope
to sustain us?

there will be no honey morning
no afternoon pollination ballet
your silence begets silence
but we are always listening

This world may have started with a bang,
crescendoed in a hum,

but it ends with

Of Restless Wonder

by Nicholas Yandell

"Do you ever feel restless?"
Asked the worker of a drone.

"Long to live beyond the structures
The hexagons of honeycombs?

Ever feel we're something more
Than antenna twitches
And wing flicks
And buzzing bands of yellow
In vast washes of green
Under distant blankets of blue?

Away from the queen
Apart from the hive
Beyond existing,
To simply survive?

Give into the urge

Disengage our tracks

Stray far from the path

And head for the horizon?"

This wisp of a quandary
Tossed out casually
By some quiet voices
Going unnoticed
Say for one small set of ears:

A passing goat who feels
Without fully comprehending
That they've never been alone
In their quest to know:

What's beyond the fences?

The long golden sheets
Spanning squinted-eye reach
The high mounds
Brushing against the clouds
The distant color explosions
And transitional motion
Of a glowing globe
Ascending the highest trees
Illuminating borders
And realms of their keepers:

Whose modest life is sketched out
Growing seeds
Tending an apiary
And watching the goats at play.

While dreaming of other lands
And faraway adventures
Of a world unknown.

The deep seas and winding rivers
Towering mountaintops and desert expanses
By automobiles and railroad cars
Airplanes and ocean liners
And that of the slick-suited travelers
Boarding massive shiny rockets
And blasting off skyward…

Those starry-eyed gravity defiers
Thrusting metal through the atmosphere
Longing to merge with specks of light
Satiating that need to go
Past the bounds
Of an earthly home
Thriving
In the warmth
Of speculation:

Like all the great explorers
Even those within the mind

Wandering the limits
Embracing imagination
Contemplating consciousness
And in what state
Or what place
Dwells life and reality.

Spiraling questions
Musings of possibilities
Spun with theories of frequencies
And desire for the ability
To commune with nature
With all the plants and animals

Even insects…
Like that little bee:

To fathom the secrets they keep
In the spans of their being
And what they too ponder
When casting out their wonder.

Return to Honey Castle
by Lily Walsh and Josh

Estranged from my family, I was surprised at the call.

"Master Anders?" said the voice. There was a distinct buzzing, what might have been electrical interference or perhaps–

"Yes? Yes? Hello," I said. "Yes. This is Anders. Hello?"

The voice on the line began a coughing fit. He had covered the receiver with his hand. By the sound, like dislodging a peppermint candy from the bottom of his throat, I knew it was the voice of my childhood butler. "There," he recovered. "There is a train ticket under your door." He began coughing again.

An envelope was slid under my door.

"Ulrich," I said. "What's happened? What's going on?"

"There is a problem in your family," he said.

"Has there been a death?" I said.

"Get on the train," he said. "Your driver is waiting."

I looked out my window. The black car outside Halpin's started and the window rolled down. A man in a black bowler hat leaned out and tapped on his watch.

I got into the car, then onto the train. Into the final car, I broke into a sweat. I spoke to my father fifteen years ago, my mother seventeen. I cannot remember my sister's or my brother's voice. And I am certain I have several aunts and uncles, but even at my utmost concentration, aided by the rhythmic clanking of the train, I could remember nary a face nor name.

The car stopped. A man as tall as a doorway opened my door. He wore a top hat and bowed to me, indicating Honey

Castle, a Gothic revival villa in the style of Strawberry Hill, only charcoal black, crooked, and obscured by dead trees.

"It is good that you have come, Master Anders," said Ulrich. "It is an unprecedented time, Master Anders."

We bypassed the front door and took the stone path through the garden. "How are mother and father?" I said.

"Dead, sir," said Ulrich. He vigorously massaged his throat.

"Oh," I said.

Ulrich was older than either of my parents. He opened the back gate, and we came to the vista overlooking our Honey Castle's hundred-acre property. It was poppies as far as the eye could see. Bees, like starlings, took the flowers in swaths. Their hum was like putting your head in a thresher.

"There is no one to tend the bees," said Ulrich.

"Tomas?" I said, my brother.

"Hospitalized," said Ulrich.

"Katarina."

Ulrich shook his head.

"Uncle Jonas," I said, their names coming back to me.

"Died tragically."

I stared into the lines of my hands. Surely, there must be others.

"You are the sole heir left living, conscious, or of sound mind." Ulrich gestured at the infinity of poppies, and the shadows of bees hanging about them.

I have had as little to do with bees as possible for twenty years. I moved to Newark to avoid all contact with flowering trees, beekeepers, or bees. I do not touch honey.

Ulrich took me to my room, with an intricate honeycomb ceiling and carved detailing to the furniture so every drawer handle is a polished echinacea or wildflower. I closed the blinds of my window—a view of the poppies. I loosened my tie and untied my shoes.

Ulrich waited patiently by the door. "Might I suggest, sir," he said. He opened the closet and searched through a number of dark-red wood chests my father brought home from India. He removed a tall white garment of thick fabric and a wide brimmed hat with thick veil—a beekeeper's suit. "Your suit, sir," said Ulrich.

I stood among the poppies. I moved slowly. A bee can smell fear. Every step I squeezed my bee smoker, Ulrich behind me squeezing his. "Your lead, sir," he said.

We approached one of the hives which lined the poppy fields, Honey Castle like a storm cloud loomed behind us. I slid a honeycomb from the hive and showed it to Ulrich. "Good show, sir," he said. He took it and set it on our small white wheelbarrow, then gave me a fresh drip tray to replace it.

I swiped at the bees gathering about my veil and slid out a second honeycomb and handed it to Ulrich. "Yes, look at that. Really nice, sir. Beautiful."

We went about it that way, removing full honeycombs and replacing them with new trays until Ulrich hefted the wheelbarrow, full now of honeycombs, up toward the castle. "I'll just take these back," he said. "We'll take next from that hive there."

"That hive?" I said.

"Yes," he said. "Is that a problem?"

It was so full of honey it leaked honey from its seams. The air about the hive wavered like gasoline vapor; the bees looked almost silver and the way they flew, well, it seemed they flew upside down.

"Will that be a problem?" Ulrich said again, lowering the wheelbarrow.

I looked at the other hives. I blinked my eyes. I wanted to rub them, reset them. I looked again at the strange bees and made eye contact with one. "No!" I said. "No, it should be no problem." I felt cold, shaken, as if woken up in a snowstorm.

"Wonderful," said Ulrich. He picked up his wheelbarrow and pushed it to the castle.

I approached the strange bees, which only grew stranger. I noticed now they flew not only anatomically as a strange species of bees, but seemingly together, in a trance, in a consistent ring around their hive, like a rotating halo.

Even their hum was strange. Fatigued perhaps from the train ride, I mistook it for a drone of words. "*Come,*" I thought I heard. I came closer, closer to the hive.

No, it was my fatigue from the train and two car rides. I took a break. I waited for Ulrich. I paced through the poppies and examined other hives. Though I had avoided this place for twenty years, it wasn't so bad. I will admit bees are frightening. But in a bee suit, it's not so bad. And, squeezing the bee smoke, I felt calmer still.

"*Come, Anders.*"

I turned to the strange bees. They continued in their strange halo. "Anders," they said.

I approached them. I put my hands on their hive.

"Hello, Anders," they said.

I lifted a honeycomb.

"It's ok," they said, now more clearly than ever. "You can take off your helmet."

I set the honeycomb in the grass against the hive, then removed and set my helmet in the grass beside it.

"Yes, Anders! That's the ticket!"

I lifted my arms, and they came to sit on them.

"Do you know what we do?" they said.

"You make honey," I said.

They climbed higher on my arms, which had begun to grow heavy. "What intelligence, Anders. Yes!" they said. "Yes, that is precisely what we do. Now try some."

The inside of their hive was so beautifully golden. I took off my gloves. "Can I?" I said, my finger ready above their hive.

"Please, Anders. Do," they said.

Their buzz grew with my excitement. We were all watching my finger. I scooped up so much honey it streamed down my hand. "Yes, Anders. Go," they said in almost a whisper.

I brought it to my mouth. My tongue recoiled from shock. It was like nothing I ever tasted. My whole body swelled with sweetness. Immediately, I was filled with energy. I could lift the wheelbarrow over my head. I could run through a mile of poppies.

"We are nightmare bees," said the bees. They were now close to my ears, as if what they said was secret.

"Nightmare bees?" I said.

"Yes, Anders. We terrify your kind to death. We distribute fear through honey."

I felt a weight grow inside my chest. Honey Castle grew taller than ever, an entire mountain with all its trees made black, the manor's terrible façade staring at me like a crooked face.

"Anders," they said.

"Yes," I said.

"Each family member before you, your brother, your mother, your sister, your father has tried to stop us and kill us, so they have each met their own terrible end. Do you want to be put into a coma, Anders?"

"No, I don't," I said.

"Do you want to be killed?"

I felt as if young children crawled quickly through the grass to tear at my legs. "Of course not," I said. The black trees swayed. My lungs compressed. The bees knew everything about me.

"Will there be a problem?" Ulrich said. He had appeared with a fresh wheelbarrow.

"No, Ulrich," I said. "I foresee no problem."

Lightning flashed, but there was no rain.

House of Honey

by Michael Santiago

A billowing plume of dust raged across the sprawling grassland. Darkness gripped the sky as the black blizzard waged onward towards the Oklahoma expanse. Since 1930, the swirling storm of dust and dirt has cascaded over fertile farmland, devastating crops and ways of life across Boise City. With an absence of land to graze, men turned to life elsewhere. The population dwindled, with those who remained questioning their stance. In the fields near Broward Street, Hank was not one of these men. He was brazen, formidable, stoic. The harsh, dreary conditions couldn't persuade him away from the home he built following the great war.

He was considered a man's man. The epitome of masculinity in a time when strength and courage was required. Most of the denizens of Boise City warned Hank that the conditions would be everlasting and worsen, yet he was not persuaded. The dust bowl did persist. It continued to destroy land and eradicate fertile crops. Dozens of livestock suffered, but even more people succumbed to the inhospitable conditions this perpetual dust storm caused. Hank was stern. The elemental horrors did not dissuade him. His son, Roderick, would often question his decision to stay, and occasionally try to guilt trip him into leaving. Hank remained; he stood his ground. He was from a time that manufactured unflinching valor, and from an era where being a man meant exerting a firm will despite the odds.

This mentality came from two defining elements in his life: his time fighting through the trenches in Gallipoli, and when his wife passed from Tuberculosis. Gallipoli, the trenches, was utter chaos resulting in lives lost across all fronts. He realized quickly that men who leaned into emotion were the first to go. His upbringing and military conditioning did instill such a distinct thought process, but his learned experience in that battle rang true. Every time. It was the same. Those who hesitated, those who leaned into fear, those who sympathized were the first to lose their lives.

But when he came back from the battle, he knew he couldn't pass on the horrors of war onto his wife, Lilith. He grew less callous towards his humanity. His wife needed him in those months before she passed, as did their son, Roderick. The boy was stricken with the early stages of cerebral palsy. As Hank fought the trenches in distant lands, Lilith held the fort at home. Battling a life-threatening condition, while caring for and protecting Roderick from the incessant bullying in town.

Three fortnights since Hank's return from the war, she succumbed to her illness. Her dying wish was for Hank to remarry and be happy, but more importantly, to care for their son until his last breath. He didn't waiver and promised her as she gasped for air one last time.

The years following her death were painful to say the least, as trauma induced nightmares smoldered within, and the death of his beloved looming over his conscience daily. The promise she made had to be kept. Truth be told, Hank didn't have enough time to foster a bond to the one similar to his mother and Roderick had no.

Nonetheless, Hank knew in the years to come he'd have to rebuild the home that was broken by the death of his wife, and to make a solid life for him and Roderick. As the years surmounted into the height of the dust bowl, Hank and Roderick cultivated farmable land, and raised livestock on the family farm he left behind for Gallipoli.

When the dust bowl swept through, Hank met his first formidable foe since the Ottoman Empire in the dank trenches in Turkey. His time fighting alongside the Australian and New Zealand Coalition (ANZAC) was troublesome and grueling, yet the years ahead proved that the terrestrial rage of dust storms proved to be a conundrum he was unprepared for.

For the last three years, these perpetual dust storms consumed light and blanketed the small town with perpetual darkness. The relentless tide of dust disrupted the way of life for Hank and his boy. A bold move had to be made.

Would he give in to nature's onslaught, or would he stand his ground and build anew?

The question rattled in his mind for weeks until he recalled a conversation he had with another farmer months back, Tommy.

Tommy was a servant of God and slaved over his crops with his father most of his life, but when the storms came, it all changed. His faith swung like a pendulum and his fields were consumed by dust. His land became infertile, so he decided it was time to flee east and create a new life for himself. He credited the revelation to Christ, as he came across the connection that the bee was the emblem of his savior. It signaled forgiveness and justice. And so, he relied on the power of God to catapult him far away from the relentless dust storms.

Hank wasn't a religious man. How could he be after all he had lost?

But he listened to Tommy explain that he was going to start his venture of being a beekeeper in Georgia, far from the grips of the dust bowl. He took notes of the appropriate items needed for an apiary and the methods to cultivate a thriving business made of honey.

As Hank reminisced on that conversation with Tommy, he looked over to his son and said, "I think I've got it."

"You mean we here are finally gone leave these god forsaken lands?" Roderick asked.

Hank, stern and ready to hunker down at the next black blizzard ready to decimate the farm, looked over at his son and stated, "We need to figure this here thing out. Our crops have been ravaged the last three years, and our livestock have been torn asunder. This whole thing needs to switch up."

"What does that mean, pa?" Roderick replied.

"It's time to switch tactics. I don't think this here farm is sustainable any longer. Our livestock are dying. We can't leave though, as I made a promise to your ma," he said.

"Then what, pa?" Roderick spoke.

"Well, Tommy left east to Georgia. Far past Boise City who figured the path forward may be opening an apiary. That may be our next path, boy," he responded.

"Pa, what the heck is that?" Roderick asked.

"We're gone be beekeepers. We can conceal it. Hide it. Hell, we can possibly sustain this. Honey for money. That's what we're going to do, boy," he replied.

"And ya think that's gone work?" Roderick inquired.

"It has to..." he stated.

Handing a list of items to Roderick, Hank explained some of the items he needed could be gathered at Carl's Supplies, the only shop in town that would have all the items he needed. He handed over the keys to his busted, oxidized Chevy pick-up and asked his son to acquire the items he needed before sunset. Roderick shrugged as he believed that his father knew best. He never questioned his dad and admired his stoic nature from within.

Roderick, bound to the use of makeshift crutches, hobbled over to the rust bucket to head into town. He hadn't been to town since his father withdrew him from school due to the incessant bullying from the Milford gang. Two years had swept by since then, but he knew he couldn't let his father down.

As he pulled into town, he drove past a couple of the kids from the Milford gang, but they didn't seem to notice him as they were preoccupied with looting an abandoned storefront. They took advantage of the calamity that struck Boise City and snatched everything they could to turn a profit for themselves. They were indurated, apathetic to the plight the residents had faced. The ongoing disaster was the catalyst for them to become ruthless.

However, not every shop owner fled; Carl's Supplies remained and was one of the businesses left during the dust bowl. Akin to Hank, Carl also made a name for himself as being a calculating and decisive figure after serving in the Great War. He had a decent relationship with Hank and knew his son Roderick, and he was aware that Hank was as hardened as he was.

Roderick pulled into the lot, clutching onto the side of the truck to gain his footing. As he clasped his crutches, he doddered into the shop to grab the supplies on his father's list.

"Ha, Roderick, is that you? I haven't seen you in eons, boy. Come here and tell me how your pa is doing," Carl shouted.

Offering a shy wave, Roderick replied, "well, as one can imagine the storms ain't too forgiving on simple folk like us. Even by the grace of God we come out unscathed. But pa, he has this idea he thinks will keep the money comin. That's why I'm here."

Handing over the list, Carl nodded and said, "Yep, I can do this. We should have all of this in stock. You just hang tight, and I'll gather what ya need."

Outside, a few boys from the Milford gang were shouting, "Look at this piece of shit. Who in their right mind would drive this junk?"

Roderick overheard the commotion as his gaze shifted outside the window and then back over to Carl gathering supplies.

"Umm, are you almost done Carl?" Roderick yelled.

"Just grabbing the last thing," Carl shouted back.

Shattered sounds of breaking glass could be heard outside, and with each piece splintering, Roderick's heart beat grew harder. He had a history with these vagrants, which led to his father assaulting one of the boys and pulling Roderick out of school. It was the best way to keep him safe, as his cerebral palsy had worsened over the years and became a point of contention for him and was the primary cause of the bullying. It didn't help that Roderick had a severe stutter anytime he felt afraid.

Carl tapped Roderick on the shoulder and said, "Here ya go, son. Now everything should be here, and don't worry about payment. These times have been tough for us all and your pa is a good man. I just hope you two can make something despite this hellscape we're living in."

"G… go… gosh Carl. Th… th… thh… thank you," he stuttered.

Walking towards the door, his hands trembled inconsolably and his heart beat harder and heavier. The sounds of chaos could still be heard outside, enacted by the Milford gang. As he managed to make his way to the car, he started the ignition, which caught the attention of the gang.

"Oh, so look here boys. This is the asshole who drives this rust bucket," one boy stated to the others.

"Ha ha… do you know who this is fellas?" a boy much larger than the rest asked.

As they started walking towards the truck, the large boy stated, "It's Roderick."

"D… Den… Dennis. I… I'm just here," Roderick said as his stutters intensified.

"Ddddd… dddd… here for what, fucker? To get your ass beat now that your dad ain't around?" Dennis antagonized.

Dennis, the leader of the Milford gang, and a few of his cronies were now standing right next to the car window. Dennis issued a series of insults, which incited hysteria among his crew, and then he began slapping Roderick's face.

Another boy grabbed the sack of supplies from the bed of the truck and began dumping them onto the lot. Several of the items scattered about the ground including a few jars of honey.

Panicked and terrified, Roderick quickly put the car in reverse, driving over Dennis' feet, and raced back to his father's farm. His eyes swelled with tears as he spoke to himself, "P… p… pa. I'm sorry."

As he drove up, he opened the door and collapsed, yelling for Hank.

Upon hearing his son, he bolted over and picked him up. "What happened, son? Tell me," Hank inquired.

"I… I… lost the supplies. It was Dennis," Roderick answered.

"You mean that prick from the Milford gang? That boy hasn't learned, has he?" he prodded.

Back in town, Dennis was on the ground tending to the bones that cracked in his feet from the two-ton Chevy. His goons looked on in bewilderment as the boy they bullied stood up against their leader.

"Boys, we are gonna pay back that son of a bitch, and teach his dear ole pa a lesson, too," Dennis yelled.

"Now pick me up and pick that shit that dumbass left behind," he yelled once more.

One of the boys began picking up the assortment of items and the jars of honey. Dennis shouted, "Hey, don't honey burn easy?"

Another boy spoke, "Sure does, boss."

"Gather round, boys. This is what we're gone do. We are going to that boy's farm come nightfall and burn that house to the ground using this here honey, which means we're going now," Dennis stated grasping the jar of honey.

It was evident that some of the boys seemed uneasy with the decision Dennis had made, but nonetheless, the sheep blindly followed as the wolf schemed. The crew helped Dennis into the bed of a truck, loaded up the supplies left behind, and began driving toward the farm.

Nightfall quickly fell and the faint sound of engines bolted across the rural landscape. The Milford gang began closing in on the farmhouse, with an unsuspecting father and son cleaning after supper.

"Pa, do you hear that?" Roderick asked.

The bustling gurgle of engines grew louder and louder as the gang got closer. Then, they stopped directly in front of the farmhouse and placed their high beams on in unison. Blinding rays of light peered through the curtains.

Hank ran to the living quarters and grabbed his Winchester from above the fireplace. "Get upstairs now," he shouted to his son.

Dennis and his crew had jars of honey in hand as they began setting them on fire and threw them towards the second level of the house, where Roderick was told to go. Makeshift honey molotovs became the tool of unwarranted vengeance. Each jar of honey shattered as the flames danced across the rooftop.

Hank ran outside and began firing his rifle at the gang. Placing well directed rounds into a few of the boys.

However, the sounds of screams resonated through the upper level where Roderick was. The entire floor was consumed by the insatiable fire ignited by the honey. Looking back, Hank saw his son desperate for help amid the inferno. He swiveled and aimed his rifle once more, shooting Dennis directly between his eyes. As the boy's body plummeted, the surviving gang members hopped back into their vehicles and drove in the other direction.

When Hank ran back inside his home, the entire second floor began collapsing around him. The floorboards gaped and turned to ash, but he could still hear his son crying for help. Hank made haste to climb up to the top level using a gutter outside Roderick's window. He shimmied his way up as the roof began to splinter into ash, yet he kept climbing. It was seemingly impossible, but Hank got to the room and guided his son towards a hay bale to jump onto.

"Son, you must jump. There's no choice. I'll be right be-hind you," he assured.

Roderick fell directly onto the hay bale and turned around to see if his father followed. Right as Hank was about to jump, the section of the roof he was on collapsed and he fell onto a pile of viscous honey from one of the jars. The nearby flames trickled toward his position, igniting Hank instantly. Roderick crawled towards him in hopes of saving his father, but as he drew near, his father muttered, "Lilith would be proud of you."

Desperate to save Hank, Roderick saw the life from his fa-ther's eyes fade as he turned into a husk swarmed in fire and honey.

The Queen Bee, A Fairytale
by Laura Scott

The Scene: A small Bavarian town in the Georgian Era
The Players:
    Georgina, the youngest sister
    Phillipa, the middle sister
    Fredericka, the oldest sister
    The Ants of a Hill
    Some Ducks
    A Hive of Bees and their Queen
    Three prince brothers, who all looked exactly alike

Phillipa and Edwina laid on a blanket in a field overlooking the river. Privileged, shiny, and wanton, the sister princesses had been avoiding their duties all week. The king and queen had even sent out a messenger to find them, but they devoured him almost immediately, plying him with wine, usurping any will he might have had to accomplish his task, having their way with him, and then sending him off in the direction of the forest, with a sore head and wobbly knees. So, the girls remained hidden in the landscape, bright in the sun, drunk with elderflower wine.

"I'm bored," Phillipa told her sister, her arm resting over her eyes, shielding the mid-morning sun.

"What shall we do?" Fredericka answered. She thought for a moment. "If we go to the tavern, they'll just alert Mother and Father."

"We're supposed to be out seeking our fortune. Perhaps we should sleep and then set off tomorrow."

This made good sense to both of them, and they rested for the remainder of the day.

By the next morning, all plans had been forgotten and

they continued to swim in the shallow river, lay in the grass, and imbibe the local friar's good floral concoction. They decided not to travel out.

Meanwhile, back at the castle, the king and queen had grown tired of their older daughters' propensity for disorder and pulled the final trick out of their royal hat: The youngest princess. They sent Georgina off to look for her sisters and to bring them home. Younger by five years, she was a different girl from Fredericka and Edwina in every way imaginable. She was kind where they were indifferent. Her common sense lay beneath every decision she made, and it seemed at times as if she could never be wrong, nor could she ever have fun. By far the most striking of the three sisters, with green eyes, dark skin and black hair, she was also the smallest, with a diminutive stature that belied her large presence.

She agreed to do this work, because it made sense, and she set off to find her ridiculous sisters. After several hours, visiting the tavern and the cake shop, she found them by the river.

"Come home at once," she demanded, looking around at the detritus of three days' indulgence spread around the meadow where the girls sat.

"Hard pass, Gigi." Edwina looked lazily up at her youngest sister.

"Yeah, I don't think I'm comfortable with that, Geege," Federicka agreed.

"Mother and Father have said they will cut you off without a penny and marry you off to two of the older Konigsburg princes if you two don't sort yourselves out."

"They wouldn't! They're, like, middle aged!" Fredericka was especially horrified. She had managed to dodge marriage the longest.

"I think they would," Georgina stared back at both of her sisters.

"Aren't they our cousins?" Edwina raised an eyebrow, disgusted.

The next morning, the three girls set off, Fredericka and Edwina to begin their journey to find their fortune and avoid the despicable option of an arranged marriage, and Georgina to get them on their way without further distraction. They walked along the river bank on a path that soon left the village behind them.

They walked for several hours until the two older princesses got hungry.

"I'm hungry," Edwina whined.

"Me too," Fredericka complained.

"Alright, let's get the blanket and the food out," Georgina started to look around for a good flat spot, but Edwina had already spread the blanket just where she stood. "Here, then. Fine," she said.

They pulled out the chicken legs and boiled eggs and carrots and parsnips and began eating. Soon the blanket was covered with ants. The ants crawled on from every direction. They covered the grass. They walked toward the girls' legs. They marched toward all of the food.

Edwina and Fredericka screamed and shrieked, stamping their feet and hopping up and down, all at the same time. Edwina took her bottle of elderflower wine she had been drinking from and began pouring it all over the ants.

Georgina put the food back in the basket, took up the blanket to give it a good shake, and looked underneath. A mound in the earth seemed to grow before her eyes, with more and more ants flowing from it. They had been sitting on an ant hill.

"We're sitting right on top of their home. It's no wonder they've all come out. Stop stomping and let's move our picnic away from here." Georgina was, as ever, frustrated by their absurdity.

That evening they made camp by the river, sitting by a fire Georgina had laid, and eating a simple dinner. As they were finishing their meal in silence, a raft of ducks came paddling by, curious about the newcomers on their banks. They looked closely and quacked. They spotted bread. They quacked more.

"Gigi, make them stop," Edwina exclaimed.

But the ducks began to paddle to the shore. They began to walk up onto the grass. They got closer and closer to the girls.

"Ah! Ducks!" Fredericka shouted and began throwing large chunks of the bread at the ducks. Edwina joined her, lobbing fist-sized pieces of sourdough at the black-backed birds. But the ducks were undeterred, and they began to eat the bread with their blue bills.

"Stop!" Georgina cried. "You'll kill them with pieces that large!" And sure enough, one went back to the river with a large piece stuck in its bill that it could neither swallow nor let go of. The duck turned on its side in the water. Georgina ran into the water, fished the bread out of the duck's mouth, who returned then to the shore. She began to pick up the pieces on the bank and break them into smaller bites for the birds. She was growing more and more tired of her sisters' antics.

The next morning, the princesses continued on their journey, wondering how much further they would have to go before they found a way to make the older two girls' fortunes. They walked for miles along the river, past villages, past orchards and more meadows. They came to rest that night just outside the grounds of an imposing castle.

Georgina went off to find berries for their dessert later, and left her sisters with instructions to build a fire for dinner. She returned to find the fire lit, which was impressive to say the least, but positioned at the base of a large oak tree, which was not.

"Oh, for heaven's sake," she said to herself.

They cooked their dinner and began eating when they noticed a few bees alighting all around them. More and more came, and Georgina looked up into the oak tree and found that a hive just above the fire's smoke was swarming.

"Bees!" Edwina yelled.

"Yes, bees, Edwina," Georgina rolled her eyes. "And your fire is going to suffocate them. Let's get it out."

Fredericka and Edwina ran as far as they could, but Georgina stayed to put earth from the riverbank on the fire to quickly smother it. The bees went back to their hive, and Georgina was more exasperated than ever with her sisters and looked forward to the moment when she could return home.

The next morning, they set off again, walking toward the edge of the castle grounds. As they approached, they noticed how quiet it was. There were no gardeners, no workers, no family to be seen. Curious, the two older sisters walked around to the other side of the castle wall. There was no one to be seen. They passed through the gate and entered the courtyard. Georgina had been a few steps in front of them and did not see them leave the path. It was several minutes before she looked back and realized she would have to turn around and look for them, once again.

The sisters found the stable and walked toward it, remarking on how everyone must have been out. Surely, horses would make some noise. They poked their heads in the first stall. Stunned, they found a horse that was gray and still. It was made of stone. Haunted, the two sisters stepped back and away slowly. They noticed that all of the stalls had the same gray, silent stone horses in them.

Georgina found them walking backwards, their eyes large and their mouths silent.

"What is this place?" she said, looking around.

"I don't know, but I'm going inside." Fredericka dashed up the stone steps into the side entrance, leaving her sisters no option but to follow.

They wandered around the castle from silent, oversized room to room. No one made a sound and there was no movement. Eventually, they found a small room off the kitchen. A shuffling sound could be heard inside. They opened the door.

"Hello! And who do we have here?" A little gray man welcomed them heartily. "I've not seen anyone in so long."

"I'm Fredericka, and these are my sisters, Edwina and Georgina." Fredericka made her status as the oldest sister known. "We are traveling to find our fortune and avoid an arranged marriage."

"Ah, lovely. Well, you must stay for supper. I've already made more than I can possibly eat." As the sun was getting lower, and the girls were a bit hungry, they agreed, and he showed them to the kitchen, where he would lay a simple table and produce a meal for them. "I haven't had anyone to talk to in some time."

The girls all looked at each other. No one said a word.

They ate in silence, saying only "thank yous" and "yesses" to the little man's queries about extra portions of the stew he had made. They finished their meal, said their goodbyes, and returned to their camp for the night, leaving him to his washing up.

The next morning, they returned to say goodbye, but found only a stone table in the courtyard. On the table was a message etched, and Fredericka, the oldest of course, read it out loud:

Complete these tasks and your fortune you shall find:

One, find and gather Prince Otto's thousand pearls, scattered in the woods.
Two, collect the key to Prince Conrad's bedchamber from the river.
Three, identify the youngest prince, Rupert, from the three identical sleeping princes.
Fail these tasks, and to stone turns your body and mind.

"Let's get this show on the road!" proclaimed Fredericka. "Edwina, you and I will start with the pearls. Which way is the forest?"

Georgina watched as they set out. She set out a plan, and as she thought and thought, the day drew long. By dusk, the sisters had not returned. Georgina walked to the edge of the forest. She looked in but could spy nothing unusual. She ventured further and found the floor of the woods glowing with tiny white lights: pearls. They were everywhere. She walked on. In the middle of the path ahead, she spied two unmoving objects. Her sisters. They were stone, gray and quiet.

Georgina was not surprised, nor could she leave them to this fate. So, she walked back to the edge of the woods. In her mind, she tried to think of a practical solution to collecting such a scattered treasure. She took some time, and as the sun sank lower and darkness was nearly upon her, the lights in the forest shifted. They began moving toward her. She watched closely as pearl after pearl began to make their way to her. She held out her skirt, as one thousand ants, coming to her rescue after she had come to theirs, delivered and deposited the one thousand glistening pearls into it.

She made her way back to the courtyard, placing the pearls in a bucket below the table. The first item on the list disappeared. She looked at the second. This was a task she didn't think she could manage alone. In the near-dark, she walked to the edge of the river. She had no lantern, but even so, it might have been impossible to find such a small thing in such a vast amount of water. She sat on the bank for a moment, watching the ducks. After some time, she noticed one swimming carefully toward her, while all the rest slept with their heads carefully nestled. The duck swam to the shore, walked up the bank toward her, and dropped a key at her feet.

"Thank you," she said, simply.

She took it back to the courtyard and deposited it on the table. The second task disappeared from the list. For the third task, she knew she would have to venture into the castle. She took the key with her. She made her way to the fourth floor and found the last bedchamber.

The key opened the door without effort, and she went in. All of the brothers looked exactly alike. All were handsome, of course, but all were sleeping. They had not been turned to stone, but they would not awaken.

Georgina wondered how she would determine who was who, when she saw a note on the bedside table of one of the brothers. It said that the oldest had eaten a bit of sugar before he slept, the middle had had some syrup, and the youngest a little honey. She thought about how to resolve this dilemma for some time, when a queen bee flew in through the open window and went straight to the brother in the middle bed.

Georgina knew this had to be the youngest brother. She touched his hand, and the spell was broken.

The princes woke up, the sisters returned from the forest, and the little gray man made them all a late dinner.

At the end of the summer together, the older princesses agreed to marry the princes, securing their fortune, but only because they wanted to.

Fredericka married Otto, the oldest prince, and they spent many lazy days complaining together.

Edwina married Conrad, the middle prince, and they moved away to a sunnier climate, where they would have even less work to be responsible for.

Georgina decided not to marry Rupert, the youngest, but instead, stayed on at his castle with him. They set up beekeeping, and a market stand. Because they had such good fortune, they simply gave away the honey and beeswax candles. The drone of the honeybees and the sweetness of their honeymaking kept the villagers, and the prince and princess, content for all of their days.

XOXO, Candyman: a Creative Latin Composition Inspired by Clive Barker's "The Forbidden"

by Heather Hambley

Cuppediatoris[1] voce coloribusque bomboque corporis cum Helena paene defigebatur[2], exsultationi tamen repugnabat. *Monstrum* erat sub ostentatione venustā, cuius nidus novacularum cruore madefactus in pedibus Helenae iacebat. Dubitet fauces eius incidere, si manum ei iniecit[3]?

Duobus Helenae hunc horrorem spectantis cordis palpitationibus[4], Cuppediator lodicem exuit.
Cum fugere ex sinibus nitebatur, iacca diloricabatur atque illa vidit — sensibus recusantibus — quae insunt pectoris putuisse et compleri iam alveo apium cavum[5]. Apes in trunco examinabant et circumdederunt reliquias carnis haerentis, aestuans turba[6]. Iste[7] manifestae illius aversationi arrisit. 'Dulcia dulcibus,' susurrabat[8] et manum hamatam ad faciem tetendit.

Cuppediator illam aggressus est. Murmurabat ea minationem ineptam quam iste neglexit. Magnitudo bombi in corpore crescebat. Horribile erat cogitatum hominis tangendi[9] propinquitatisque insectorum. Illa sursum arma[10] graviora plumbo impellebat, ut istum sustineret[11]. Os horrendum in pariete imaginem[12] obscuravit. Ut istum tangeret, illa animum inducere non poterat, regressa est autem. Stridor apium magis magis[13] fiebat; aliquae excitae fauces ascenderant atque ex ore erumpebant[14]; circa labra capillosque repebant.

Helena identidem istum orabat ut eam omitteret[15], sed iste non placabatur. Denique nihil latebrarum[16] ei superfuit; paries fuit a tergo. Obdurescens contra aculeos ponensque in trunco aestuanti palmas, ea trusit. Simul manus istius circum cervicem evolavit atque uncus rubicundam faucium cutem perstrinxit. Illa sanguinem rorantem sensit; persensit istum ictu terribili iugulaturum esse. Fidem vero iste dederat atque praestetit. Apes suscitatae in omnia miscebantur[17]. Illa sensit eas moventes et quaerentes in auribus frustula cerae saccharumque in labris. Alapam dare eis non omnino conata est. Uncus fuit in cervicem. Si illa se ex loco moveat, vulneretur[18].

Illaqueata est, sicut in pueritiae somniis, omni effugii spe elusā. Cum somnus eam ad talem desperationem tulerat — daemonibus undique discindere exspectantibus — ultimus dolus ei suberat. Dimittere[19]; deponere omnem vitae cupiditatem relinquereque corpus tenebris. Ut Cuppediatoris facies in faciem Helenae premebat et bombus apium spiritum delebat, illa manum occultam lusit[20]. Sicut in somniis, cella nefariusque erasi sunt atque evanuerunt.

Special thanks to Allie Pohler.

---

[1] For the name of Candyman, I formed my own noun from *cuppediae*, 'candy' by adding the *-tor* suffix to denote an agent. I wanted *Cuppediator* to sound friendly and innocent on its face, similar to Candyman.

[2] *cum...defigebatur*: *cum* is delayed in this concessive cum-clause; cf. Apuleius, *Metamorphoses* 3.22, where the protagonist Lucius becomes transfixed as he witnesses the magical transformation of the witch Pamphile into an owl. I used the same verb *defigere*, which can be translated literally as, 'to fix, root to the spot,' and more figuratively, 'to bewitch, enchant,' to reflect both the physical and figurative power that the sight of Candyman has over Helen.

[3] mixed conditional, with a past simple protasis and future less vivid apodosis

[4] I placed Helen taking in the horror (*hunc horrorem*) of Candyman within the ablative of time (*duobus...cordis palpitationibus*) to reflect both the quickness of her reaction, as well as a certain suspension of time.

[5] *quae insunt...putuisse et compleri...cavum*: indirect statements; note the chiasmus and relative time of the perfect infinitive *putuisse* and present infinitive *compleri*.

[6] *aestuans turba*: in apposition to *apes*; I wanted to contrast the static nature of Candyman's clinging flesh (*carnis haerentis*) with the dynamic life of the bees' seething mass (*aestuans turba*). This also highlights Candyman's isolation compared to the collective consciousness of bees.

[7] "[*Iste*] especially refers to one's opponent (in court, etc.), and frequently implies antagonism or contempt" (Allen & Greenough 297c). I felt conflicted using forms of iste for Candyman because I think of him as an exceptionally sympathetic character given how his backstory and character have been developed in both the *Candyman* (1992; 2021) movies. I ultimately opted to use *iste* to represent him as Helen's adversary, though, as he's depicted in Clive Barker's original short story, which is focalized through Helen.

[8] I incorporated onomatopoeic language throughout the composition to mimic the buzz of the

bees that Helen hears from the very beginning of her encounter with Candyman (e.g., *bombo, susurrabat, murmurabat*).

[9] genitive gerundive with *hominis*

[10] a little wordplay here to reflect the battle between Helen and Candyman; see also the military language throughout (e.g., *compleri, circumdederunt, regressa est, effugii*).

[11] *ut…sustineret:* purpose clause

[12] *Imagines* can also refer to death masks worn in Roman public funerals to honor the dead and reanimate their ancestors with their likenesses depicted in wax. Compare to how the graffiti of Candyman keeps him alive in present memory and leads to his appearance in the story.

[13] cf. Verg., *Georg.* 4.311

[14] cf. Verg., *Georg.* 4.313. In *Georg.* 4.281-314, Vergil describes the fabled ritual of *bugonia*, by which a new beehive is spontaneously brought to life from a young ox carcass, beaten to death for this purpose. I wanted to play around with the relationship between life and death here. The beehives in both stories are a result of great violence. In the *Georgics*, the eruption of bees from the dead bullock is a sign of new life; whereas, when the bees burst out of Candyman's mouth (*erumpebant*), they bring death and destruction for Helen…or perhaps of the new life Candyman promises in her demise.

[15] *ut…omitteret:* indirect command

[16] partitive genitive with *nihil*

[17] cf. Verg., *Georg.* 4.311

[18] future less vivid conditional

[19] *Dimittere, deponere, relinquere* are all infinitive subjects.

[20] I preserved the idiom *manum occultam lusit,* 'she played that hidden hand,' even though it doesn't have a Latin counterpart, because each word connects to the larger story and signals a role-reversal for Candyman and Helen. Up to this point, we've been focused on Candyman's literal hands, but here I used *manum* figuratively to describe Helen's *ultimus dolus*. Although she can't fight Candyman in physical combat, she can parry his attack psychologically. I chose *occultam* here because Candyman's torso of bees was originally concealed by his jacket and then revealed, to Helen's horror; now the focus moves to Helen's hidden knowledge. As for *lusit*, I like that it transplants childlike language into horror, as with Candyman's name. Candyman has been toying with Helen throughout the story, but with Helen as the subject of *lusit*, the verb signals a shift in power.

Glossary

aculeus, -i, *m. sting*

aestuo (*1*), *to seethe, surge; to be excited, be in heat*

alapam dare (*c. dat*), *to slap*

alveus, -i, *m. beehive*

animum inducere ut (*c. subj*), *to bring oneself to, convince oneself, make up one's mind*

apis, -is, *f. bee*

arma, -orum, *n. pl. arms, weapons*

arrideo, -ēre, -risi, -risus (*c. dat*), *to smile at*

a tergo, *at one's back*

aversatio, -onis, *f. repugnance*

bombus, -i, *m. buzzing, humming*

capillus, -i, *m. hair*

caro, carnis, *f. flesh*

cavum, -i, *n. hollow*

cella, -ae, *f. small room*

cera, -ae, *f. wax*

cervix, -icis, *f. neck*

circumdo, -are, -dedi, -datus, *to enclose, surround; (in war) to encompass, besiege*

compleo, -ēre, -evi, -etus, *to fill, impregnate; (in war) to bring (a legion) to full strength*

conor, -ari, -atus, *to try*

cresco, -ere, crevi, cretus, *to grow, increase; to swell*

Cuppediator, oris, *m. Candyman*

cutis, -is, *f. skin*

deleo, -ēre, -evi, -etus, *to blot out, extinguish*

depono, -ere, -posui, -positus, *to lay down; to resign, give up*

dilorico, -are, —, -atus, *to unbutton, tear open*

dimitto, -ere, -misi, -missus, *to let go, relinquish*

discindo, -ere, -cidi, -cissus, *to tear apart, cleave, rend*

dolus, -i, *m. trick, deceit*

dubito (*1*), *to hesitate*

dulcis, -e, *sweet*

effugium, -i, *n. flight, escape*

eludo, -ere, -si, -sus, *to foil, to outmaneuver*

erado, -ere, -si, -sus, *to scratch out, erase, obliterate*

erumpo, -ere, -rupi, -ruptus, *to burst forth, break out*

evanesco, -ere, -nui, *to vanish, die away*

evolo (*1*), *to fly out, fly up*

examino (*1*), *to swarm*

exsultatio, -onis, *f. rapture*

exuo, -ere, -ui, -utus, *to throw off (clothes)*

facies, -ei, *f. face*

fauces, -ium, *f. pl. throat*

fidem dare, *to give one's word;* **fidem praestare**, *to keep one's word*

frustulum, -i, *n. morsel, mouthful*

haereo, -ēre, haesi, haesurus, *to hang, stick, cling*

hamatus, -a, -um, *hooked, furnished with a hook*

ictus, -us, *m. blow, stab, cut, thrust*

illaqueo, -are, —, atus, *to entrap, ensnare*

impello, -ere, -puli, -pulsus, *to push, wield; to urge, incite*

iugulo (*1*), *to cut the throat of*

labrum, -i, *n. lip*

latebrae, -arum, *f. pl. retreat, a lurking-place*

lodix, -icis, *f. blanket*

ludo, -ere, -si, -sus, *to play, deceive*

madefacio, -ere, -feci, -factus, *to drench, soak*

manus, -us, *f. hand*

manum inicere (*c. dat*), *to lay hands on*

minatio, -onis, *f. threat*

misceo, -ēre, miscui, mixtus (pass), *to swarm*

nidus, -i, *m. nest*

nitor, niti, nixus sum (*c. inf*), *to try to, struggle to*

non omnino, *adv. not at all*

novacula, -ae, *f. razor*

obdurescere contra (*c. acc*), *to steel oneself against*

occultus, -a, -um, *hidden, concealed, secret*

omitto, -ere, -isi, -issus (*c. acc*), *to leave alone*

os, oris, *n. the face, countenance, features*

paries, -etis, *m. wall*

persentio, -ire, -si, -sus, *to feel deeply, perceive clearly*

perstringo, -ere, -inxi, -ictus, *to graze*

plumbum, -i, *n. lead*

premo, -ere, -essi, -essus, *to press; (of sleep, death) to overcome, overpower*

propinquitas, -atis, *f. proximity, nearness*

pueritia, -ae, *f. childhood*

putesco, -ere, putui, *to become rotten*

quaero, -ere, -sivi, -situs, *to seek, look for*

quod inest (*s.*), **quae insunt** (*pl.*), *contents*

recuso (*1*), *to object, refuse, protest*

regredior, regredi, regressus sum, *to step back; (in war) to retreat*

reliquiae, -arum, *f. pl. remnants*

repugno (*1*) (*c. dat*), *to fight against, struggle with*

roro (*1*), *to drip, trickle, drop dew*

rubicundus, -a, -um, *flushed*

se ex loco movere, *to budge from the spot*

sentio, -ire, sensi, sensus, *to feel, perceive*

sinus, -us, *m. fold*

somnium, -i, n. *a dream; vision*

somnus, -i, *m. sleep*

spes, -ei, *f. hope, chance*

stridor, -oris, *m. shrill or high-pitched sound; whirring (of wings)*

subsum, -esse, *to be near, to be at hand; to be concealed*

supersum, -esse, -fui, *to be left, remain*

sursum, *adv. up, upwards*

suscito (*1*), *to rouse (from inactivity)*

sustineo, -ēre, -tinui, -tentus, *to hold back, restrain, keep back*

susurro (1), *to whisper, buzz*

tango, -ere, tetigi, tactus, *to touch*

tendo, -ere, tetendi, tentus, *to stretch out, shoot (an arrow or weapon)*

tenebrae, -arum, *f. pl. darkness, night; haunts*

trudo, -ere, -si, -sus, *to push, shove*

truncus, -i, *m. body, trunk (of a tree or human)*

ultimus, -a, -um, *final, last, extreme*

uncus, -i, *m. hook*

venustus, -a, -um, *enchanting, charming*

Bios

Ellen Austin-Li
Ellen Austin-Li's work has appeared in *Artemis, Thimble Literary Magazine, The Maine Review, Pine Mountain Sand & Gravel, Rust + Moth*, and other places. A Best of the Net nominee, she's published two chapbooks with Finishing Line Press: *Firefly* and *Lockdown: Scenes From Early in the Pandemic*. She earned an MFA in Poetry at the Solstice Low-Residency Program. Ellen lives with her beekeeper husband in a newly empty nest, overrun with books, in Cincinnati, Ohio. Find her work @ www.ellenaustinli.me.

Jan Ball
Jan has had 364 poems published in various journals internationally and in the U.S. including: *ABZ, Mid-American Review*, and *Parnassus*. Finishing Line Press published her three chapbooks and first full-length poetry collection, *I Wanted To Dance With My Father*. Orbis, England, nominated her for the Pushcart Prize in 2020 and Constellations nominated her for it in 2021.
Besides her poetry, Jan wrote a dissertation at the University of Rochester: Age and Natural Order in Second Language Acquisition after being a nun for seven years then living in Australia for fourteen years with her Aussie husband and two children. Jan has taught ESL in Rochester, New York and Loyola and DePaul Universities in Chicago. When not traveling, or gardening at their farm, Jan and her husband like to cook for friends.

Maev Barba
Dr. Maev Barba attended the Puget Sound Writer's Conference in 2018. She is a PNW native and a great lover of books. She used to sell books door-to-door. A doctor of astronomy, Barba looks into space and considers neither the small as too little, nor the large as too great, for the lover of stars knows there is no limit to dimension.

Tom Barlow
Tom Barlow is an Ohio writer of poetry, short stories and novels. His work has appeared in journals including *They Said, PlainSongs, Ekphrastic Review, Voicemail Poetry, Hobart, Tenemos, Redivider, Aji, The New York Quarterly, The Modern Poetry Quarterly*, and many more. See more at tombarlowauthor.com.

STELLA BAUER

Stella Bauer is a junior at Lindenwood University and is working towards a major in English with an emphasis in creative writing. When not studying, Stella works at a Barnes and Noble Cafe where she spreads her love for reading and caffeine. Stella enjoys spending time with her friends, family, and cats, Baxter and Hazel. Stella can often be found reading fantasy and romance books, but will read just about anything. She also enjoys writing, knitting, and dreaming the day away.

MACKENZIE BENINATI

Mackenzie Beninati (she/her) is a poet, story teller, and proud cat mom from Utah by way of Colorado. She has performed in national poetry slams and small cafes, has been published in the student literary journal *Riverrun*, and has self published chapbooks of poems about queerness, railroads, and loving yourself.

A.B. CABDRIVER

Long Beach (Washington, not California) native, Cabdriver takes inspiration from the wildlife around him, the wildlife far below him when he's out in his boat, and the wildlife he used to see as a child during his short visits to the Oregon Zoo. Cabdriver has been a writer-in-residence at the Sou'wester on fifteen separate occasions. And still nobody remembers him!

YUAN CHANGMING

Yuan Changming edits Poetry Pacific with Allen Yuan in Vancouver. Credits include Pushcart nominations & chapbooks (most recently LIMERENCE) besides appearances in Best of the Best Canadian Poetry (2008-17), Poetry Daily & BestNewPoemsOnline, among others. Yuan was nominated and served on the jury for Canada's National Magazine Award (poetry category).

JENNIFER CLARK

Jennifer Clark works part-time with Communities In Schools of Kalamazoo and over the years has partnered with librarians and bookstore owners on a number of cool projects that benefit youth. Clark is also the author of a children's book and three full-length poetry collections. Her newest book, Kissing the World Goodbye (Unsolicited Press), ventures into the world of memoir, braiding family tales with recipes. She lives in Kalamazoo, Michigan. Her website is jenniferclarkkzoo.com.

EMMY CLARKE

I am an autistic, lesbian writer and poet from Manchester. I live in Shropshire with my partner, our smelly black cat, and three rescue chickens. In 2021, I secured a place on Sophie Willan's Stories of Care writing development programme. In February 2022, I was welcomed into the Manchester Rainbow Library Project, headed by poet Jay Hulme and illustrator David Roberts.

Currently I'm studying a part-time BA in English Literature and Creative Writing, and work part-time as a Bookseller at Booka Bookshop in Oswestry, Shropshire, where I become mysteriously misty-eyed every time an anxious queer teen requests a copy of Alice Oseman's Heartstopper. My work has also been featured in: UNBURIED FABLES anthology (2016) WOMEN OF THE WILD anthology (2017), Outbox Theatre's BRIGHTER collection (2021), TALES OF THE BOLD, THE BRAVE AND THE BEAUTIFUL anthology (June 2022).

RYAN CLINESMITH

Ryan is an educator and writer who loves music and interdisciplinary arts. His poetry is concerned with poetic tradition and the nature of influence on modern writing. He works as an administrator at a primary school and routinely acquires book collections for its library.

MICKEY COLLINS

Mickey ~~rights wrongs~~. Mickey ~~wrongs rites~~. Mickey writes words, sometimes wrong words but he tries to get it write.

ESTÉE ARTS CRENSHAW

Estée Arts Crenshaw is a doctoral candidate in the department of Writing & Rhetoric Studies at the University of Utah. She received her MFA in creative writing from Brigham Young University. Estée's academic work in comparative rhetoric focuses on premodern Japanese poetry and aesthetic traditions.

JOHN DAVIS

John Davis is a polio survivor and the author of *Gigs* and *The Reservist*. His work has appeared recently in *DMQ Review*, *Iron Horse Literary Review*, and *Terrain.org*. He lives on an island in the Salish Sea.

MARK DECARTERET

Mark DeCarteret has been working at Water Street Books in Exeter NH for 10 years. Worked at Stroudwater Books in Portsmouth for 7. And Wordsworth in Cambridge MA for 1. He's also worked at the Emerson College Library in Boston and volunteered at Wiggin Memorial Library in Stratham NH. His poetry has appeared in 450 reviews, 25 anthologies and 7 books.

Doug
"doug" has been writing and drawing all their life. They found it was time to come out of their cave and share some of these creations. "doug" may or may not be a pseudonym for a person who works at a prolific Northwestern local bookstore, but feels the name "doug" represents their works just as samely as any other old name.

Rob Duisberg
Rob Duisberg is a composer and beekeeper in Seattle. He is retired from a working life in software, artificial intelligence in particular. So he came to beekeeping not for the honey, but to be in the presence of these astounding distributed intelligences. But what to do with all the honey? He has therefore also taken up brewing, and produces a fine cider with local apples, hops and honey.

Sara Eddy
Sara Eddy is the author of two chapbooks of poetry, *Tell the Bees* (A3 Press, 2019) and *Full Mouth* (Finishing Line, 2020), along with a book of ekphrastic poetry written in collaboration with the photographer Dominique Thiebaut. She has published widely in literary journals: some of her poems have appeared recently in *Threepenny Review*, *South85*, *Raleigh Review*, and *Ekphrastic Review*. She is Assistant Director of the writing center at Smith College, in Northampton, Massachusetts, and works in close collaboration with the librarians in the special collections at Neilson Library, especially on collections centered on consumerism, food & cookbooks, poetry, and beekeeping. She maintains her own collection of vintage cookbooks for use by food writing students at Smith. She lives in nearby Amherst with a teenager, a black cat, and a white dog.

Lynette G. Esposito
Lynette G. Esposito, MA Rutgers, has been published in *Poetry Quarterly*, *North of Oxford*, *Twin Decades*, *Remembered Arts*, *Reader's Digest*, *US1*, and others. She was married to Attilio Esposito and lives with eight rescued muses in Southern New Jersey.

Robert Eversmann
Robert Eversmann works for *Deep Overstock*.

Anna Laura Falvey
Anna Laura Falvey (she/her) is a Brooklyn-based poet and theater-maker. In 2020, she graduated from Bard College with degrees in Classics & Written Arts, with a specialty in Ancient Greek tragedy and poetry. She spent her college career blissfully hidden behind the Circulation and Reference desks

at the Stevenson Library, where she worked. Anna Laura has been a teaching artist with Artists Striving to End Poverty since 2019, and is currently serving as an ArtistYear fellow, teaching Poetry in Queens, NY where she is the resident teaching artist at a transfer high school. Her work has appeared in *Icarus Magazine* as well as in issues 15 and 16 of *Deep Overstock*.

STEPHANIE FLUCKEY

Stephanie Fluckey (she/her) is a writer and artist living in the Pacific Northwest. She holds an MFA in Creative Writing from Lindenwood University. When She is not writing to the sound of Seattle rain, she is reading or gardening. Stephanie is the 2022 Guest Editor of Emerging Voices in Fiction at *Oyster River Pages*. Poem 'Silent Night' published July 2021 on www.Survivorlit.org

GABBY GILLIAM

Gabby Gilliam lives in the DC metro area. Her poetry has most recently appeared in *Tofu Ink, The Ekphrastic Review, Cauldron Anthology, Instant Noodles, MacQueen's Quinterly*, and *Equinox*. You can find her online at gabbygilliam.squarespace.com or on Facebook at www.facebook.com/ GabbyGilliamAuthor.

LYDIA GWYN

Lydia Gwyn's stories, poems, and essays have appeared or are forthcoming in *F(r)iction, The Journal of Compressed Creative Arts, The Florida Review, Elm Leaves Journal*, and others. She is the author of the flash fiction collections *Tiny Doors* (2018, Another New Calligraphy) and *You'll Never Find Another* (2021, Matter Press). She lives with her family in Tennessee, where she works as an instruction librarian at East Tennessee State University.

HEATHER HAMBLEY

Heather loves horror and Latin, so this project was a dream. She studied Latin at Reed, taught for 4 years, and now writes Latin compositions for fun. Her all-time favorite scary movies are The Wicker Man and Jennifer's Body. She currently lives in Central Oregon with her husband Andy and their 15yo doggo Mo. Heather's website is latinklub.wordpress.com.

BROOKE HOPPSTOCK-MATTSON

Brooke Hoppstock-Mattson is an American poet living in Canada with her spouse and ginger cat, David Bryne. When she is not writing, she is collecting honey & salmon for her day job. Brooke has work published in *the borderline* and forthcoming in *First Literary Review – East*.

Julie Jones

Julie Jones earned her MFA from the Vermont College of Fine Arts. Her stories have appeared in the *Chicago Quarterly Review, Doctor T. J. Eckleburg Review, Cincinnati Review: miCRo,* and *Burningword Literary Journal,* among others. Her work has been nominated for Best Microfiction 2020 and Best of Net 2020. She writes early mornings before attending to her duties as a federal court law librarian. You can find her at juliemjones.com.

Alshaad Kara

Alshaad Kara is a poet who writes from his heart. His poems were published in an anthology, "PS: It's Still Poetry - An Anthology of Contemporary Poetry from Around the World" and a journal, "The Suburban Review Issue #25: Juice".

Melissa Kerman

My name is Melissa Kerman and I'm a writer from Long Island.

Rae Lamicq

Rae Lamicq is a writer, mother & educator who lives in Oregon. She has been a Youth Services Reference Assistant at both Cedar Mill Community Library & Beaverton City Library. She currently does on-call work at BCL. Her poems for this issue were inspired by a delightful text she read on all things apiary: *A Short History of the Honey Bee: Humans, Flowers, and Bees in the Eternal Chase for Honey* by E. Readicker-Henderson. She checked it out from the library.

Karla Linn Merrifield

Karla Linn Merrifield has had 1000+ poems appear in dozens of journals and anthologies. She has 15 books to her credit. Following her 2018 *Psyche's Scroll* (Poetry Box Select) is the full-length book *Athabaskan Fractal: Poems of the Far North* from Cirque Press. Her newest poetry collection, *My Body the Guitar,* recently nominated for the National Book Award, was inspired by famous guitarists and their guitars and published in December 2021 by Before Your Quiet Eyes Publications Holograph Series (Rochester, NY). She is a frequent contributor to *The Songs of Eretz Poetry Review*. Web site: karlalinnmerrifield.org/; blog at karlalinnmerrifield.wordpress.com/; Tweet @LinnMerrifiel

nat moon

nat moon is a visual artist living in los angeles with their partner, kiddo & pup. they are lucky enough to be married to a true curator and steward of books, and look forward to sharing their love of books with their kiddo (& pup.)

Timothy Arliss OBrien

Timothy Arliss OBrien is an interdisciplinary artist in music composition and writing. He has premiered with The Astoria Music Festival, Cascadia Composers, and ENAensemble's Serial Opera Project. He has published several books of poetry, (*The Art of Learning to Fly, Dear God I'm a Faggot, Happy LGBTQ Wrath Month*), and has written for Look Up Records (Seattle), and *Deep Overstock*: The Bookseller's Journal. He also hosts the podcast The Poet Heroic, and manages the digital magic space The Healers Coven.

He also showcases his psychedelic makeup skills as the phenomenal drag queen Tabitha Acidz.

Check out more at: www.timothyarlissobrien.com

Rebecca Patrascu

Rebecca Patrascu works as a library associate for the Sonoma County Library. Her writing has appeared in publications including *Smartish Pace, Glint, The Shore, Bracken Magazine, Prairie Schooner, Colorado Review*, and *Valparaiso Review*. She has an MFA from Pacific University and is the author of the chapbook *Before Noon*. She catches honeybee swarms in the spring.

Katherine D. Perry

Katherine D. Perry is a Professor of English at Perimeter College of Georgia State University where she teaches writing and American Literature. Her first book of poetry, *Long Alabama Summer*, was released in December of 2017 from Finishing Line Press and draws heavily on her childhood experiences on the Alabama Gulf Coast. Her poems have been published in journals such as *Writers Resist, The Dead Mule of Southern Literature, Poetry Quarterly, Southern Women's Review, Bloodroot, Borderlands, Women's Studies, RiverSedge, Rio Grande Review*, and *13th Moon*. She is also a co-founder of the Georgia State University Prison Education Project, which brings college courses to incarcerated students in Georgia prisons. She lives in Decatur, Georgia with her spouse and two children and identifies as a Southern writer, even when that label is complicated. Her website is www.katherinedperry.com.

Mary Salome

Mary Salome (she/her) is a queer Arab- and Irish-American writer and media activist who lives in San Francisco with her partner, their dog, and some semi-feral cats. She has produced radio, video, and web publications, and is currently a Digital Communications Supervisor at the University of California San Francisco. Her prose and poetry have been published in *Sojourner Magazine, Food for our Grandmothers: Writings by Arab-American and Arab-Canadian Feminists, Tiny Seed Journal*, and *Instant Noodles*, among other publications. Though it might complicate her brand, she is also ordained in the Triratna Buddhist Order.

Michael Santiago

Michael Santiago is a serial expat, avid traveler, and writer of all kinds. Originally from New York City, and later relocating to Rome in 2016 and Nanjing in 2018. He enjoys the finer things in life like walks on the beach, existential conversations and swapping murder mystery ideas. Keen on exploring themes of humanity within a fictitious context and aspiring author.

Laura Scott

Laura lives south of Portland, Oregon with her Irish husband, all-seeing, all-knowing teenage daughter, and her sock-stealing dog, Pluto. She makes her living as a college composition instructor, helping others to write.

Bob Selcrosse

Bob Selcrosse grew up with his mother, selling books, in the Pacific Northwest. He is now working on a book about a book. It is based in the Pacific Northwest. The book is *The Cabinet of Children*.

Jihye Shin

Jihye Shin is a Korean-American poet and bookseller based in Florida.

Lauren Swift

Lauren's work has appeared in or is forthcoming with *Cimarron Review, Denver Quarterly, North American Review, Atlanta Review, The 2River View, The Rumpus, Birdcoat Quarterly, No Contact,* and *Poets.org* as the recipient of Academy of American Poets Prizes in 2016 and 2019. You can find her online at www.laurenswift.com.

Jonathan van Belle

Jonathan van Belle is a philosopher and author, most recently of *Zenithism* (2021) from Deep Overstock Publishing. His forthcoming book, *Be Not Afraid of Life: In the Words of William James*, with co-author John Kaag, will be published by Princeton University Press in early 2023.

Z.B. Wagman

Z.B. Wagman is an editor for the *Deep Overstock Literary Journal* and a co-host of the Deep Overstock Fiction podcast. When not writing or editing he can be found behind the desk at the Beaverton City Library, where he finds much inspiration.

Lily Walsh

Lily Walsh lives south of Portland, Oregon where she has just completed her first year of high school. She is the author of *Zombie Mountain*, *The Worry Wart*, *Stories!*, and the forthcoming, *Penguin Party* published by Pluto House.

Nico Wilkinson

Nico Wilkinson (they/them) is a poet, bookmaker, and farmer living in Colorado Springs, CO. They are the founder of the Keep Colorado Springs Queer open mic. They co-founded Prickly Pear Printing, which publishes anthologies of queer love, joy, and growth and incorporates letterpress and linocut printing techniques. Their home, The Queer Artists in the League of Love (Quaill) Club, has housed over 15 LGBTQIA+ artists and writers. They are always trying their best.

Nicholas Yandell

Nicholas Yandell is a composer, who sometimes creates with words instead of sound. In those cases, he usually ends up with fiction and occasionally poetry. He also paints and draws, and often all these activities become combined, because they're really not all that different from each other, and it's all just art right?

When not working on creative projects, Nick works as a bookseller at Powell's Books in Portland, Oregon, where he enjoys being surrounded by a wealth of knowledge, as well as working and interacting with creatively stimulating people. He has a website where he displays his creations; it's nicholasyandell.com. Check it out!